"Give it time, Mark.

"You'll soon have your life back in order," Alice said in reassurance.

She laid a hand on his arm, and he covered it with his.

She was standing closer to Mark than she should be, Alice realized, and she tried to remove her hand and move away. But Mark held her with a firm grip.

"For the first time in months," he said softly, "I actually believe that. When you came to us, I felt as if a burden had been lifted off my shoulders. I can't understand it. You walk into our house, and suddenly I'm confident that all my troubles are over. Why is that, Alice?"

"I don't know, Mark," she whispered. "But I'm glad it's so. Because it feels right for me to be here...."

Books by Irene Brand

Love Inspired

Child of Her Heart #19
Heiress #37
To Love and Honor #49
A Groom To Come Home To #70
Tender Love #95

IRENE BRAND

This prolific and popular author of both contemporary and historical inspirational fiction is a native of West Virginia, where she has lived all her life. She began writing professionally in 1977, after she completed her master's degree in history at Marshall University. Irene taught in secondary public schools for twenty-three years, but retired in 1989 to devote herself full-time to her writing.

In 1984, after she had enjoyed a long career of publishing articles and devotional materials, her first novel was published by Thomas Nelson. Since that time, Irene has published twenty-one contemporary and historical novels and three nonfiction titles with publishers such as Zondervan, Fleming Revell and Barbour Books.

Her extensive travels with her husband, Rod, to forty-nine of the United States and thirty-two foreign countries, have inspired much of her writing. Through her writing, Irene believes she has been helpful to others, and she is grateful to the many readers who have written to say that her truly inspiring stories and compelling portrayals of characters of strong faith have made a positive impression on their lives. You can write to her at P.O. Box 2770, Southside, WV 25187.

Tender Love
Irene Brand

Published by Steeple Hill Books™

STEEPLE HILL BOOKS

Steeple
Hill™

ISBN 0-373-87101-5

TENDER LOVE

Visit us at www.steeplehill.com

Printed in U.S.A.

O Lord, you have searched me and you know me....
Where can I go from your Spirit?
Where can I flee from your presence?
—*Psalms* 139:1, 7

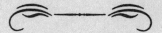

O God, you have searched me and you know me...
Where can I go from your Spirit?
Where can I flee from your presence?
—Psalm 139:1-7

Chapter One

The Tanner home stood in sharp contrast to the other dwellings along the suburban Richmond street. Other lawns were neat and the houses in good repair, but the wooden trim and the front door at the Tanners' needed a paint job. Draperies at the picture window sagged haphazardly. The shrubbery obviously hadn't been trimmed last season. Blooming red and white geraniums peeked forlornly over the weeds that had taken over the brick planter along the curving sidewalk.

Alice Larkin drove by the two-story brick house three times before she had the nerve to stop. Betty was right, Alice thought. This family does need help. It was amazing that a short visit to her friend in Richmond would offer an unexpected opportunity to be of service.

Alice questioned just how far she should go to help out a family in need. For a moment she was tempted to drive on, return to her well-ordered life and forget she'd ever heard about Mark Tanner and his family. Instead, she turned her van into the drive-way and breathed a prayer before she turned off the ignition.

"God, I've never felt Your leading so strongly in any phase of my life. If it's Your will that brought me to this point, I pray for direction because I don't have any idea what I'm facing."

Her friend, Betty St. Claire, director of a local nanny agency, had set up the interview for Saturday morning when all of the Tanners would be at home. When she rang the doorbell, Alice wondered which family member would answer her ring. The door was opened by a slender girl, dressed in a blue sweat outfit. The girl's dark hair accentuated her pale skin and blue eyes.

Eight-year-old Kristin. Betty had described her as a shy, soft-spoken girl.

Kristin observed Alice with anxious eyes.

"I'm Alice Larkin. I have an appointment to see Mr. Tanner."

The girl unlatched the storm door. "Come in," she said softly. "He's waiting for you."

Kristin beckoned to Alice, and she followed the girl down a short hallway until she paused at an open door.

"The lady's here, Daddy."

Alice walked into the untidy office just as a man, dressed casually in jeans and a blue sweater, rose from behind a littered desk and came toward her with outstretched hand. Kristin turned quickly and entered a room adjacent to the office.

"I'm sorry, Mrs. Larkin, that I wasn't at the door to meet you," he said and pressed her hand with a firm grip. He motioned toward the desk. "I've been doing book work this morning and time got away from me. I'm Mark Tanner. Please have a seat.''

Alice sat down, gladly. Betty's brief physical description hadn't prepared her for Mark Tanner. Betty had said he was a forty-year-old widower, but she hadn't said that he had thick, wavy hair as black as a crow's feathers, neatly trimmed to his nape. Nor had she mentioned that his eyes were as blue as a cloudless cerulean sky on a crisp October afternoon. Gray streaks of hair glistened above his ears, and his smooth, fair skin was marred only by a deep dimple on his right cheek. The only flaw Alice found in Mark's appearance was that he was much too thin for such a tall man.

"Did Betty explain our family situation?" Mark asked in a deep and pleasant voice.

"Just the basics—she didn't give me many details," Alice said somewhat breathlessly, wishing for a few moments to recover from the shattering blow her heart had suffered. What was there about this man that affected her so strongly? If she came to work here, she couldn't have her emotions stirred this way.

"My wife, Clarice, died six months ago, leaving me with two children. You met Kristin just now, and Eddie, my five-year-old, is a sickly child. I need someone to care for them while I work. I've tried two daytime nannies, but it hasn't been satisfactory. I'm sometimes late getting home, and often the nanny would be gone several hours, leaving the children without any supervision. Although we're crowded for space, I asked Betty to recommend a live-in nanny.''

"Don't you have an older woman living here?"

"Yes—my wife's grandmother, Gran Watson. Clarice was her nearest relative, and she came to live with us three years ago after she had a stroke that partially paralyzed her. The children need more supervision than she's able to provide."

While Mark gave a few more details about his family, Alice recalled what Betty had said about his affairs.

"Mark Tanner," Betty had said, "has had enough trouble to ruin any man. His son was born with a congenital heart defect, that required a series of expensive operations. Over two years ago, his wife was diagnosed with uterine cancer, and she died in December after a downhill battle all the way. He's a brilliant man and served as pastor of our church for ten years, but he resigned about a year ago because he couldn't fulfill his obligations to the church while he looked after his children and nursed his wife. He'd built up a good retirement fund in our church organization, and when he resigned, he withdrew the capital to take care of his living expenses. By the time Clarice died, he was on the verge of financial ruin— he still owed on his son's medical bills, Clarice's health needs had been expensive, and when he tried to pay those bills, his other obligations fell behind. After her death, he went to work in a bank, and so far he's kept his home, but I've heard he may lose it. You might be his last hope."

"That's preposterous. I'm not a magician. How could I make such a difference?"

"You can take care of his children and make a home for him. If he doesn't have to worry about the daily care of his children, he can devote more time to his work."

No wonder he looks tired, Alice thought, but she wished that Betty hadn't placed such a guilt trip on her. If she didn't come to work for him, and Mark lost his long fight to remain solvent, would she always blame herself? But her reaction to Mark's magnetic personality was an immediate red flag, for she was sure a good nanny shouldn't be personally involved with any member of the household.

"Perhaps you should tell me about yourself, Mrs. Larkin," Mark said, with a smile that caused her heart to move in a way she hadn't experienced before. "Where is your home? Do you live in Richmond?"

"No, I've lived in Alexandria since my marriage ten years ago. I'm a native Virginian—I was born in Spotsylvania County."

He smiled again, and the dimple deepened. "I guessed that from your soft accent. How much experience have you had as a nanny?"

Alice laughed lightly. "None! Although I haven't worked as a nanny, I'm not a novice where children are concerned. I taught for three years in a kindergarten before I married. And prior to his death, I spent several years caring for my ailing husband, so I know quite a lot about children and illness, which seem to be the qualities you need in a nanny."

"How long have you been a widow?"

"My husband died over a year ago as the result of a rare liver ailment. I've thought of teaching again, but while I was here in Richmond visiting Betty, whom I've known since my college days, she suggested that I might enjoy being a nanny."

Actually, Betty's appraisal had been a bit more blunt.

"You'll go nuts if you don't get out of that house and start living. Even if you do have all the money you'll ever need, you should go to work. John Larkin was a fine man, and although I still can't imagine why you married a man so much older than you, you've done all you can do for him. You need a life of your own."

"And what do you have in mind?" Alice had answered, with only a hint of pique. She had learned long ago that Betty's blunt manner hid a heart filled with concern for others.

"I have a client who needs immediate help," Betty said, "and I've checked all my applicants without finding the right person. Let me tell you about Mark Tanner," Betty said, and her comments had spawned Alice's interest in the Tanners.

Mark smiled encouragingly, and Alice continued, "Perhaps you should tell me what you expect from a nanny."

"I suppose it boils down to the fact that I just need a housekeeper." He waved his hand around the room. "The whole house is a mess, mostly because there's no organization." He threaded his thick hair with long, shapely fingers. "There's no way I can work full-time, be a parent, and take care of this house and property. I'm sure the neighbors are ashamed of the lawn, although they've been kind enough not to say so, but I can't afford to hire a gardener, and I don't have the time. School closes next week for the summer, and I must have someone to supervise the children. I need so much that I hardly know where to begin. Why don't you tell me what you're willing to do?"

Instinctively, Alice wanted to rush to Mark, put

her arms around him and tell him that she'd shoulder his whole burden. Careful, Alice! She told herself.

"Mr. Tanner, I believe it's customary for a nanny to work five days a week and have the weekends free, which might be a satisfactory arrangement for you. Also, Betty says that you and I should agree on my workload, benefits, and salary. Right now, however, I don't know what any of that should be."

"I don't mean to complain because I've been in tight spots before and have always managed, but right now, I'm having trouble making ends meet. However, that won't make any difference in our financial arrangements, for the children are my major priority, and I want to provide the best care possible for them. Betty seems to think that's you."

Alice lowered her eyes from his warm gaze and fiddled with the purse in her lap.

"Perhaps I could come to work on a trial basis? I suggest that I come for a month at a nominal salary. I'll take care of the cooking, housekeeping, and child care. During that time, you can see how I fit in with your family, and I can determine what needs to be done. At the end of the month, we can evaluate the situation—if you've found my work satisfactory and I'm contented, then we can talk about contract terms."

"That sounds like a one-sided agreement, Mrs. Larkin—all in my favor."

"Perhaps not," Alice said, with her slow smile. "I may be a lousy cook, for all you know."

The telephone rang, and Mark answered.

"Kristin, it's for you," he called, and Kristin tiptoed in. She took the phone and moved to a corner of the room.

"I suppose the first thing is for you to look over the house and meet the rest of the family," Mark said.

Kristin put her hand over the mouthpiece of the phone.

"Daddy," she said, "Susie wants to know if I can go to church camp with her next month?"

Mark's face flushed, and he said, "What would it cost?"

"Seventy-five dollars."

"Oh, Kristin," Mark said, "I don't see how you can." He motioned to the stack of bills on his desk. "I've explained all of this to you. By next year, I'll be able to provide extras like that, or perhaps you can go to another camp later on in the summer. For now, I'll have to say no. Sorry."

"That's okay." In the phone, she said, "Not this time, Susie. Maybe next year. Bye."

"You aren't getting a good opinion of our family," Mark said, as he stood, and Alice thought his smile came with an effort. "Shall we tour the house?"

The downstairs consisted of the kitchen and dining area, living room, a large family room, Mark's office, a powder room and an enclosed back porch, seemingly a repository for odds and ends. The family room with its deep chairs, bookshelves, a large table covered with magazines and children's books, a comfortable couch, and large entertainment center was the most attractive room on the first floor.

Upstairs, were four bedrooms and two baths. Alice was introduced to Gran Watson, an eighty-year-old, who had little use of her left hip and leg. Gran's voice had been affected by the stroke, and she spoke with a lisp through a partially paralyzed mouth.

Eddie was a scrawny five-year-old, with a colorless face and a weak voice. Dark curls covered his head, and his blue eyes were dull. His room was small, housing a set of bunk beds, a dresser, and a collection of toy automobiles. He lay on the bed watching a television cartoon, showing little interest in his potential nanny. Kristin followed Alice and Mark from room to room, listening intently to everything they said.

When they returned to Mark's office, he said, "I'll expect you to take my room, and I'll move in with Eddie."

Alice shook her head. "Not at all," she objected, envisioning Mark's cramped position in the narrow bunk bed. "You wouldn't get any rest that way. Why can't I sleep on the porch? If we move some of those cartons and use that extra bunk bed in Eddie's room, I can manage all right—at least through the month's trial period."

Mark agreed reluctantly.

"Since I expected to be away only a few days when I left Alexandria, I'll have to return home to get some more clothes and put my affairs in order for an extended stay. Will it be convenient if I start working a week from Monday?"

"Yes, we can manage until then."

As Alice prepared to leave, she asked, "How much authority will I have over the children and the household? If I have to get your okay every time I need to make a decision, your burden won't lift at all."

Mark's blue eyes looked long and intently into Alice's brown ones, and she met his gaze unflinchingly. At last, he reached for her hand. "My primary concern is for Kristin and Eddie, and I believe I can trust you with the welfare of my family—that's all I'm concerned about at this point."

He squeezed her hand and walked with her to the car.

"If you need to contact me, Betty will know where I am," Alice said, and waved to him as she backed out of the driveway.

An hour later, sitting in Betty's office, Alice paced the floor and gave Betty her impression of the Tanners, excluding only her physical attraction to Mark.

"My hands were itching to pull back the draperies, wash the windows and let some light into those rooms. And on a nice day like this, both Kristin and Eddie should have been outdoors, not cooped up in the house. How sick is Eddie, anyway?"

"As I understand, surgery has completely repaired the damage to his heart, and he's able to resume a normal life. You can find out from his father or pediatrician what he's able to do. I don't believe Mark will give you any opposition. He's the best organized preacher we've ever had at our church, and it must frustrate him to see his household in such disorder, but he's simply in over his head."

"I suppose that's the reason I decided to help him."

"But let me caution you, Alice. I know *you,* and you'll want to move in there and expect an overnight miracle. It won't happen that way. Their home life has been going downhill for two years—you won't change it in a few days."

Alice shook her head despairingly. "You're right,

and I'll try to go slow. But there is something I can do. This morning, a friend telephoned Kristin and invited her to go to church camp. Mark had to refuse because he couldn't afford it, and I want to provide that money anonymously. Will you handle it for me?"

She reached in her purse and removed seventy-five dollars.

"No problem. I'll put the money in a blank envelope, mark it for Kristin Tanner's camp expenses and drop it in the offering plate Sunday. No one will ever need to know."

Alice paused in her pacing to straighten a picture on the wall. "I'm not completely at ease with this situation, Betty. It's quite a responsibility, and I'm afraid that I'll get too involved with the family's problems. You know I've always wanted children of my own. What if I get attached to Eddie and Kristin? It will hurt when I have to leave them."

"That's a risk all nannies take, and some of those listed with my agency have been hurt." Betty observed Alice as she stood looking out the window, and she said compassionately, "But, Alice, why don't you remarry and have children of your own?"

"I don't intend to marry another man I don't love. I couldn't have found a more considerate, kinder husband than John Larkin, but I didn't love him, and I haven't seen any other man I thought I could love." Mark's brilliant blue eyes set in his charming face flashed through her mind, and she didn't look at Betty, fearful that her friend might note the truth in her face.

Betty, a happy wife and proud mother of three, was a noted matchmaker. She took Alice by the shoulders and turned her to face the full-length mirror on the wall behind her desk.

"Look at you," Betty said, and she enumerated Alice's features as if she were announcing a beauty contest. "Honey-blond hair, pink-and-white complexion, finely chiseled features, with a smile that always seems to be lurking in steady brown eyes, while also possessing a firmly molded attractive body of above medium height."

Betty released Alice's shoulders and perched on the desktop. "You're wasted as a single person. You *must* get married again."

"When I'm ready, I'll tell you," Alice said, with a laugh.

Betty's face became more thoughtful. "Although your chief role at the Tanners is to care for those children, I'm concerned about Mark, too." She paused and rolled a ballpoint pen back and forth on the desk. "I've never known a more effective preacher, and he should be in the ministry—not working in a bank. It was a blow to our congregation when he resigned, and the membership would have taken him back immediately when Clarice died."

"He didn't ask for a leave of absence when he left the church?"

"No. He wouldn't take one when the official board offered it. And while he said he couldn't come back to the church because he needed a lucrative job to take care of his debts, I've wondered if that's the real reason."

"Well," Alice said, "I'll have to admit when I was so confined with John's illness and couldn't see any hope for the future, there were times when my faith faltered. We've all been in that position."

"That's true, but the doubts eventually fade away. Yet in Mark's case, I don't think they have."

Once back in her own home, Alice's mind became an emotional pendulum. One moment she'd think, This move is definitely God's will for my life; then she'd fret, Why can't I be satisfied with the status quo?

In spite of her doubts, she kept on packing her minivan with clothing and personal items to make her life more pleasant at the Tanners'. As she made arrangements to close her house for a few months, she questioned why she would even consider leaving her comfortable life-style, her spacious three-story brick colonial home, her church friends and her relatives to assume the responsibility of another's family, to sleep in a bunk bed on a porch, and take on household duties that she paid to have done in her own home.

When she prayed for wisdom, God led her to a verse in the Psalms, "I will instruct you and teach you in the way you should go; I will counsel you and watch over you."

That was the only assurance she had that her decision was the right one, for a visit to her parents, Harley and Norma Taylor, who lived in a retirement community in the nation's capital, wasn't encouraging. Norma couldn't understand why her daughter would want to take on a nanny position.

When Alice had inherited all of John's assets, her parents took it for granted that they were also recipients of his money, and were never hesitant about asking for financial help. They thought that if Alice wanted to take care of children, she should devote her time to her niece and nephew, children of Nancy, Alice's single-parent sister, who always had financial needs.

Alice took comfort from her prayers and continued packing.

She timed her arrival for Sunday afternoon, and when she reached the street where the Tanners lived, she compared her present sangfroid to her nervousness the week before.

Mark opened the door before she had time to ring the bell. His wavy hair was tousled, there was a black smudge on his face, and he wore an apron over his jeans with a message printed in flashy letters, What's A Nice Guy Like You Doing In A Dump Like This?

"You did come back," he said, and the relief expressed in his eyes and on his face reinforced her belief that it was right to be here.

"What made you think I wouldn't?" she said in her low voice, as he held the door for her.

"I couldn't blame anyone for hesitating to take on a job like this one," he said with a slight laugh.

"In my own strength, I wouldn't have tackled it, but Mr. Tanner, I believe God is calling me to this position."

Mark's face darkened, and he ignored her comment.

"You're in time to join us for a late lunch, early dinner or whatever. I'm grilling hamburgers in the backyard. We're about ready to eat. Gran and Kristin are making lemonade. I was going upstairs to bring Eddie down when I heard your car drive in."

When Mark turned toward the stairs, Alice walked

into the kitchen. "Anything I can do to help?" she asked after she greeted Gran and Kristin.

"You can carry out the lemonade, if you like," Gran said in her halting voice. "I need both hands for my walker, and the pitcher is a bit heavy for Kristin."

"We've got your room ready, Mrs. Larkin," Kristin said. "Want to see?"

"Sure."

Alice walked with Kristin to the porch. The miniblinds were closed, and the room was cool. One corner was piled high with boxes, but the rest of the room had been cleared for her use, and a small chest, chair, table and bunk bed moved in.

"Is the room all right?" she asked anxiously, reminding Alice of a troubled adult.

"I'll be very comfortable here. I brought my own television, and a few other personal items that I'll move in later."

"Daddy says you're only coming for a month."

"Maybe longer, if we get along all right."

"Guess what!" Kristin said excitedly. "I'm going to camp next week. Daddy couldn't afford to send me, but someone at the church provided the money."

"That's great," Alice agreed. "I'm sure you'll enjoy church camp—I always did when I was a girl."

When they returned to the kitchen, Mark was entering with Eddie, stooping low with an arm around the boy to support him. Eddie shuffled along like an old man.

Alice carried the iced beverage, Kristin picked up a package of hamburger buns and a bag of corn chips and they followed Mark and Eddie out to the yard, where hamburgers sizzled on the grill. Gran awkwardly maneuvered her walker down the two short steps, but Alice didn't offer to help because she gathered that Gran wanted to maintain as much independence as possible.

The backyard was larger than the small weedy area in front of the house, and it was secluded from the neighboring houses by a tall wooden fence that required a coat of water seal. Shrubs needed a good pruning, and the grass was sparse in spots, while weeds grew profusely. A huge evergreen shaded the lawn, littering the whole area with pine needles. A wooden picnic table was situated on a stone patio beside a gas grill sending out tempting aromas.

"Kristin, will you bring the carton of potato salad from the refrigerator?" Mark said as he settled Eddie into a chair. With a dimple-deepening grin at Alice, he added, "I bought it at the deli—I'm not a cook and wouldn't have time to prepare food if I was."

"What can I do to help?"

"Not a thing," he insisted. "This meal is on me. You don't start work until tomorrow."

Alice sat in an aluminum folding chair and sipped the lemonade that Kristin brought her.

"What should we call you?" Kristin asked.

"I'd like for you to call me by my first name— Alice."

The hamburger was overdone and ketchup dripped around the edges of the bun, but Alice ate it, as well as the large pile of corn chips, and scant portion of potato salad that Mark served.

"I'm tired, Daddy," Eddie whined before Mark had time to eat anything. "I want to go back to my room."

"Can't you eat anything else, Son?" Mark asked worriedly.

Eddie shook his curly head, and Mark left his plate and helped Eddie back into the house. Alice watched their departure speculatively. Did Eddie need all this coddling or had they spoiled the boy? she wondered.

Alice turned to Gran. "What is Eddie's problem? Betty St. Claire told me his surgeries had been successful."

Speaking with difficulty, Gran said, "The heart's malfunction has been repaired, but he isn't gaining much strength."

"I'll get Mark's permission to call his doctor and find out what kind of diet and exercise would help Eddie. He'll have to be stronger than he is now if he goes to school this fall."

They spent the rest of the afternoon unloading Alice's van. Mark whistled in amazement when she opened the rear gate of the van. "Where will we put all these things?"

"We'll leave most of them in boxes, and I'll unpack when I need something. I brought my television and computer, and a folding table for them, and there's plenty of floor room for that. I didn't notice a computer when I was here last week, and I thought it might be a good way to entertain the children."

"Kristin has been pestering me to buy a computer," he said lightly, "but that's another thing I can't afford right now."

"Give it time, Mark. You'll soon have your affairs in order." She laid her hand on his arm, and he covered it with his. She was standing closer to him than she should be, and she tried to remove her hand and move away, but he held her with a firm grip.

"For the first time in many months, I believe that. When you came this afternoon, I felt like a burden had been lifted off my back. I can't understand it. You walk in the house, and suddenly I'm confident that all my troubles are over. Why is that, Alice?"

"I don't know, Mark, but I'm glad it's so," she whispered. "It feels right for me to be here."

Chapter Two

Before she went to bed, Alice checked out the kitchen. While the equipment was adequate, the food supply was short, and she'd need to go to the grocery store before she did much cooking. Alice located several boxes of cold cereal, some fruit bars and a box of oatmeal that hadn't been opened. There was plenty of milk and orange juice, and a small can of coffee in the refrigerator. Although an expensive coffeemaker sat on the cabinet top, a jar of instant coffee on the table indicated that Mark didn't take time to fresh perk his coffee.

Her sleep was sporadic, and since the master bedroom was over the enclosed porch, Alice heard Mark's footsteps when he got up at six o'clock. She dressed in denim shorts and a yellow knit shirt and hurried into the kitchen. She prepared the coffeemaker, sprinkled oatmeal in a pan of boiling water, poured a glass of orange juice, and placed a plate and cup on the table. Two slices of bread were waiting in the toaster when Mark came into the kitchen.

He was dumbfounded!

"Why, Alice! I don't expect you to wait on me. I've always gotten my own breakfast."

"I was awake, and I might as well be doing something. I've cooked oatmeal. Would you like to have eggs with your toast?"

He sat at the table awkwardly, seemingly at a loss to know how to deal with the situation. "The oatmeal and toast will be fine. I don't eat a heavy breakfast."

Alice lowered the bread into the toaster, dipped up a serving of the steaming oatmeal, sprinkled a handful of raisins on it, and set the bowl in front of Mark. She placed the milk container beside his plate. "Sugar and cream for your coffee?"

"No, I drink it black. Won't you eat with me?"

"I'll have a cup of coffee now, but I'll wait to eat with the children. Do you mind if I set up a schedule for meals?"

"Make any schedule you like. I've told both of them to do what you say."

"What time do you get home in the evening?"

"Usually between five and six—but I sometimes have to stay late with a client."

"Shall we schedule dinner for six o'clock? If you're not here by then, we'll go ahead and eat."

"I'll do my best to be here as much as possible. I need that time with my family. And I'll take care of them at night, so you can have every evening free if you want to go out."

The rest of the week was an endurance test in patience for Alice. On Monday morning when she tried to get the children out of bed at half-past eight, Kristin came down reluctantly, but Eddie said he didn't want any breakfast. About ten o'clock, she heard a bell ringing, and Kristin informed her that Eddie rang the bell when he wanted something. She climbed the stairs dutifully, and when she entered his room, he said, "I'm hungry, Alice."

She looked at her watch and said, "It'll be two hours before lunch. I'll call you when it's ready. In the meantime, perhaps you should straighten up your bed and pick up some of these things on the floor. I'm going shopping this afternoon, and I want you and Kristin to go with me."

"I want something to eat now."

"Eddie, your daddy said it was all right to have our meals at a regular time. I'll have lots to do to keep your home comfortable, and I can't be serving food all day. You'll soon get used to eating earlier in the morning."

Eddie closed his eyes, drooped forlornly, and he absolutely refused to get out of his chair and tidy the room, but Alice noticed that when noon came, he hungrily ate his grilled cheese sandwich and apple, and asked for a second glass of milk.

At the end of the first few days, Alice's patience was stretched to the breaking point—the children didn't like the food she cooked, they wanted to watch television rather than play outdoors, and they hadn't been taught to look after their own rooms. Alice hesitated to push Eddie too much, until she'd spoken with Eddie's pediatrician. After she heard Dr. Zane's blunt assessment, Alice knew for Eddie's sake, she had to force him to change his life-style.

"I've told Mark," Dr. Zane said, "to quit mollycoddling that boy. In earlier years, he did have to take it easy, but the surgeries have corrected his heart problem, and he needs to be more active. To sit in

his room and watch cartoons on TV is more detrimental to his health than if he starts playing Little
League ball. Do what you can to snap him out of his
lethargy, and I'll support you.''

At the end of the first week, Alice could note some
progress. They ate meals on schedule, and while Alice did furnish some of their usual snacks, the children were also eating more vegetables and fruits.
When she weeded the flower beds, she kept Kristin
and Eddie beside her and was gratified when they
pulled a few weeds and happily reported to their father what they'd done. Eddie still expected Kristin or
Alice to come running when he rang his bell, and
when he begged her piteously to do what he wanted,
his blue eyes, so much like his father's, beseeching
and hurting, Alice found it hard to deny him anything. Although she wanted to bestow tender love on
the boy, she knew she must occasionally practice
tough love.

Fortunately, Gran Watson supported Alice.
''These children have needed a firm hand for a long
time. After Clarice became ill, she couldn't do anything, and Mark had too much on his mind to discipline his children. When they complain to me, I'll
turn a deaf ear,'' and she added with a whimsical
little laugh that Alice found endearing, ''I can't hear
very well anyway, so it's easy enough.'' Gran was
no trouble to Alice, for she cared for her own needs
and kept her room in order, and she was overly com-
plimentary of Alice's cooking.

''I used to be a good cook,'' she said, ''but I'd
lived alone for fifteen years before I came here, so I
was out of the habit of cooking, and with my handi-
cap, I haven't been up to preparing a good meal.

Mark doesn't have time to cook, even if he knew how, which he doesn't. We've been existing, and very little more.''

At night, Alice went to her room as soon as she straightened up the kitchen after dinner, closed the door, and left Mark alone with his family. When Saturday came, she was ready for a break, and after eating breakfast with Mark, she left for the day. By previous appointment, she went to Betty's house.

''You look a little harried,'' was Betty's first comment.

''It's been a hard week,'' Alice said with a laugh, as she leaned back in a lounger and dropped her shoes to the floor. ''But I've made a difference in their lives, and that was my goal in the first place. After a year of drifting, it's challenging to be needed again.''

When Betty heard all that she'd done during the week, she threw up her hands in dismay.

''Alice! You're supposed to be a nanny—not chief cook and bottle washer. You'll kill yourself with such a schedule.''

''If you were working there, you'd do the same things I'm doing. Everywhere I look, there's something important to do. My main concern right now is how to spend the money to make their lives more comfortable without Mark learning about it. Although his back is against the wall financially, I don't believe he'll readily accept help from a stranger.''

''What kind of financial help do you have in mind?''

''Nothing major. On my first trip to the grocery store, I spent more than what he'd budgeted for the month. I can get by with that, and he'll never know, but Kristin should have some new clothes before she goes to camp. She's a thin girl, but she's quite a bit taller than she was last summer, and her jeans are too short.''

"Watch the paper for yard sales, and take her to one of those. You can add a few new outfits, and Mark won't notice."

"I also want to have a professional cleaning service come in and clean the whole house. He does have a woman come in for a few hours on Thursday, but she can't keep up with all the work."

"A group of our church women has taken house cleaning as a ministry. If the family is able to make a donation, fine. If not, they clean the house free of charge. Talk to Mark about it—he'll never know how much money you give them."

"Thanks, Betty—you've solved my two biggest problems."

"Let me warn you, Alice, that Mark Tanner is an intelligent man, and he's going to realize soon that you aren't an ordinary nanny. You should tell him before he figures it out for himself."

"This is only for a month's trial," Alice reminded her. "After that, I may tell him."

"If you stay there three more weeks, Alice, you'll be hooked, and you know it. I'm your friend, and I don't want you to get hurt. I feel responsible for you since I'm the one who mentioned the Tanners to you."

Alice laughed at her. "Hey, I'm a big girl now— I can look after myself."

Betty's eyes were skeptical. "I wonder."

"By the way, who is Ethel Pennington?"

Betty grinned at her. "So you've seen her, have you?"

"I can hardly help it. She's been in and out of the house several days this week, and Wednesday, she brought hamburgers and French fries for Kristin and Eddie at two o'clock in the afternoon. I took charge of the food and told her that we'd have it for dinner—that I'd scheduled regular hours and I didn't want the children nibbling between meals. She was obviously angry, and Kristin and Eddie weren't happy about it either, but I won that battle, for so far, Mark is supporting me. Too much of that kind of food isn't good for Eddie. Dr. Zane said he needs fruits and vegetables."

"To answer your question—Ethel is a spinster who's had her eye on Mark for years. She lives a few blocks from the Tanners, and as soon as Clarice got sick, she became the ministering angel. She intends to be the next Mrs. Tanner, and she's working on Mark through the children."

"Is Mark interested in her?"

"I doubt it very much, but she isn't easily discouraged."

The night before Kristin left for church camp, Mark telephoned that he would be late getting home.

"If you don't mind, Alice, you can put the children to bed early. I don't want them staying up until I come home."

She prepared beef stew, Waldorf salad, and hot rolls for dinner, putting aside enough food for Mark in case he hadn't eaten before he came home. The children were quieter than usual as they ate, and Kristin merely picked at her food. As Alice cleared the table and filled the dishwasher, the children dogged her steps—she couldn't get a foot away from either one of them.

After her work was finished, she said, "Your father asked me to send you to bed early, for he didn't know when he would be home."

"Oh, Alice, please don't make us go to bed before Daddy comes," Kristin begged, and Eddie puckered up as if he would soon burst into tears.

"But he doesn't know what time he'll be here, and we leave for camp early in the morning."

Kristin grabbed her hand, and Eddie tugged on Alice's jeans. "But I won't sleep until he comes. When he's late, we're always afraid he's not coming home. Please, don't send us to bed, Alice. Eddie will cry until he's sick."

Like a bolt from the blue, Alice suddenly realized that she'd misjudged the situation in this home. Her whole focus had been to discipline these children, Eddie in particular, and to build up their physical bodies with the right kind of foods and exercise. And while those things were necessary, suddenly she realized that, more than anything else, Kristin and Eddie needed love and security. They'd witnessed their mother's slow death, and knowing that Mark was all they had left, their fear of losing him was overpowering.

She'd been listening to her head and not her heart. Her conscience smote her, and she put an arm around Kristin and ruffled Eddie's hair.

"You can wait up for a while anyway. Why don't you take your baths, get into your pj's, and we'll sit in the living room and wait for him? What do you and your father do in the evenings?"

A smile lit Kristin's face, and Eddie hugged Alice's legs. "We play games sometimes or sit on the couch and watch television." She giggled. "We watch the programs, but Daddy sits with his arms around us and goes to sleep most of the time."

"I should be able to handle that," Alice said. "Up the stairs with you, then. I'll help you with your bathwater, Eddie, and I'll turn down your beds so you'll be ready when your daddy comes home."

"Will you tell him we got ready all by ourselves?" Eddie asked.

"If I don't have to do too many things for you."

While she waited for them to finish bathing, Alice tried to think of a game that would interest both of them. As soon as Mark helped her set up the computer, she could provide many educational and entertaining programs for them to watch, but that wouldn't help her tonight.

Deciding there was a difference between spoiling and loving, she started downstairs. "Come down when you're ready," she called. She was mixing a pan of fresh apple muffins when they found her in the kitchen.

"I'm going to put these in the oven to bake, and we can have milk and muffins later on."

"Oh, boy," Kristin cried. "We'll like that, won't we, Eddie?"

He nodded happily and tugged on Alice's hand. She knelt beside him and smoothed back his wet hair, and he threw his arms around her and kissed her. The caress had a strange effect on Alice, for it lighted an ember in her heart that had never been touched— she had the first glimmering of what a mother's love entailed. Her voice quavered when she spoke.

"While the muffins bake, let's play a game my sister and I used to enjoy. We'll sit here at the table." On the table, Alice laid a sheet of paper she'd brought from her room. "We're going to draw creatures. I'll start first."

"But Eddie can't draw," Kristin said.

"Sure, he can. I'm going to draw the head of a dog, then you, Kristin, can add the body, and Eddie will draw the legs and feet of the dog."

"That won't be hard to do," Kristin agreed. "I make good grades in art."

"Ah, but there's a catch to it," Alice said. "Neither of you can look while I'm drawing the head, and I'll fold over the top of the paper before I hand it to you. Eddie can't watch while you're shaping the body, and you'll fold over what you've done before he draws the feet and legs."

Kristin frowned. "I don't know if I can do that."

"Let's try it anyway. Each of us will mark where the next part of the animal is supposed to be drawn. Cover your eyes."

Alice quickly sketched an outline of what purported to be a poodle, although art wasn't one of her strong points. She folded the paper so that only the edge of the neck was showing.

"Okay, Kristin, you can look now, but Eddie keeps his eyes covered."

Kristin screwed up her eyes in concentration as she carefully drew the body of a dalmatian. Watching her, Alice deduced that she did have some artistic talent. When Eddie's turn came, with his tongue sticking out the corner of his mouth, he outlined four legs that could belong on no other dog except a dachshund.

As she watched Eddie's tiny fingers painstakingly creating the legs and feet, Kristin smiled broadly, and when he finished and Alice unfolded the paper, Kristin laughed, shouting, ''That's the funniest looking dog I've ever seen.''

The head of an aristocratic poodle attached to the spotted, thin body of a dalmatian, supported by four short, sturdy legs *was* amusing.

Eddie giggled, saying, ''But I did make nice legs, didn't I, Alice?'' He jumped up and down on the chair. ''I want to draw a bird. Let me draw first this time.''

They'd made three more creatures by the time the muffins were ready, and the two children were more animated than Alice had seen them. She removed the muffins from the pan.

''Do you want to eat a muffin now or wait until they've cooled?''

''They smell so good, let's have one now,'' Kristin said, ''and maybe we can have some more when Daddy comes home.''

''We need to share with Gran. Eddie, will you take her a muffin while I pour the milk?''

He jumped out of his chair. ''I want to show her our pictures, too.'' He tucked the images they'd drawn under his arm and took the muffin Alice placed in a plastic bowl. She watched him a bit anxiously for she hadn't seen Eddie go up or down the stairs by himself, but neither he nor Kristin seemed to realize that his behavior was unusual. She waited with bated breath until he returned to the kitchen, and although his color was heightened and his breathing accelerated, soon after he sat down and started eating his muffin, his complexion and breathing were normal.

"I want to show Daddy the pictures, too," he said.

"Fine. Help me rinse our glasses and plates, and we can leave them in the sink. We might have another snack with your father when he comes home, if it isn't too late."

"But you said we could wait up for him," he said.

"Well, I didn't exactly say that, but if you do get sleepy, I'll stay upstairs with you until he's home."

When they went into the family room, before they turned on the television, Kristin said, "What's another game you and your sister played?"

"We used to tell progressive stories. One of us would think of a subject and we'd make up a story about it. The first one would talk for a few minutes, then the other one would add on ideas. We'd switch back and forth, changing the story content to fit what the one before had said until we thought the story was finished. They were make-believe stories. Think you could do that?"

"I can do it," Eddie said, "if Kristin can."

"I want to start the story," Kristin insisted.

They settled on the couch with Alice between the two children.

"Natasha was a little girl, and she was afraid of spiders," Kristin started.

"I don't like that name—I can't say it," Eddie protested.

"Make him listen, Alice," Kristin said, and turning a stern eye on her brother, she said, "You're not supposed to say anything until I've finished."

Alice put her arm around Eddie, and he snuggled

close. "If you can't pronounce Natasha, maybe you can say, Tasha."

"Tasha," he said experimentally. "I'm going to call her Tasha. Hurry up, Kristin, so I can talk."

Two stories and an hour later, Alice had learned a lot about her companions. They were both afraid of spiders, they were terrified of the dark, they couldn't understand why their mother had to die, and they were worried about the future—especially what would happen to them if their father should also die. These revelations disturbed Alice, especially when she knew that Kristin was going to camp tomorrow where she would probably encounter lots of darkness and spiders.

When the second story ended, Eddie said, "Okay—what're we going to play now?"

Smothering a yawn, Alice said, "How about the 'take a nap' game?"

"Hey, Alice, that's sneaky," Kristin said. "I bet there isn't any such game."

"No, but I'm sleepy. Let's find a show on television that you like, and you can watch while *I* take a nap."

Kristin looked at the clock. "It's ten o'clock, and we usually aren't awake this late, so we don't know what to watch." Her face twitched nervously as she added, "It's awful late, I wonder if Daddy is all right."

"I'm sure he is." *What could she say to calm the fears of these children?* "Shall I tell you a story before I take my nap?"

"Is it the kind where we talk, too?" Kristin asked.

"No, this is a Jesus story? You know who Jesus is, don't you?"

They solemnly nodded their heads.

"Once when Jesus was talking to a group of his friends, he told them they shouldn't worry about things that they couldn't change. Some of them were afraid they wouldn't have enough food to eat, others didn't think they had enough clothes. And Jesus said that they should trust God to take care of them and not worry about what might happen tomorrow."

Kristin and Eddie looked at her in mystification, obviously without any understanding of her words.

"Take your daddy, for instance. Let's say he's had a flat tire on the way home, and it took some time for him to repair it. Is there anything you can do to help him?"

"I don't think so," Kristin said slowly.

"Then why should you worry about it? Or be afraid that something terrible has happened to him? God loves your father, and He'll look after him."

"Then why did He let my mommy die?" Eddie whispered, tears glistening in his big blue eyes.

God, I'm getting in over my head. Help!

"Your mommy was very sick, wasn't she? God took her to be with Him, and she won't ever be sick again. Would you want her to still be here with you and hurting a lot?"

"No," Kristin said, "but why didn't God heal her? We need her more than God does."

"I don't have all the answers, but I know this— God *could* have healed your mother, but why he didn't, I can't tell you. We have to trust God to do the right thing, although we can't always understand why He doesn't do what we want Him to do."

"I miss my mommy," Eddie said, his chin quivering, and Alice's heart ached for the boy. She leaned over and kissed his cheek, now wet with tears.

"I know you do, but there's nothing you can do to bring her back. So instead of worrying about things you can't help, why don't you be the kind of children your mother would want you to be?"

"What would she want us to do?" Kristin wondered.

"Oh, she'd want you to help your daddy and not let him know how sad you are, and try to grow up healthy and strong, and learn a lot of things. Do you think you can do that?"

"Maybe," Kristin said, but she looked doubtful.

"Let's learn a Bible verse? There's one that says, 'I will trust and not be afraid.' Could you say that with me and mean it?"

Several times, they repeated in unison, "I will trust and not be afraid."

When she thought they had the verse committed to memory, Alice said, "Let's turn on the TV and watch one program. If Mark isn't home by then, you should go to bed." When she found a commentary on wild animals that seemed appropriate for the children to watch, she added, "I'm going to take a nap—your father will probably be here by the time the program ends."

Alice didn't really intend to go to sleep, but she thought it might induce sleep in her charges. When she awakened groggily, she slitted her eyes, noting that Kristin was lying with her head on Alice's lap, and that Eddie was snuggled against her, sheltered by her right arm. Her arm was numb, and she supposed that had awakened her until she roused further.

Mark stood over them, the remote in his hand, turning off the television.

Alice flushed to have him see her in such close proximity to his family, and she sat up, her movement awakening Kristin and Eddie.

"Daddy!" Kristin cried. "You did come home. We worried about you until Alice taught us a verse, 'I will trust and not be afraid.' Then all of us went to sleep."

Rubbing the sleep out of his eyes, Eddie wiggled away from Alice and ran to Mark. He clutched the pictures they'd drawn. "Look, Daddy—we've been drawing pictures."

"And telling stories," Kristin interrupted him. She took Mark's hand. "Come in the kitchen. Alice made apple muffins, and we saved some for you. I'll pour the milk."

"Pictures, stories and muffins, too! I'll have a hard time entertaining you from now on," Mark said to his children, but his eyes were on Alice, and she lowered her lashes against his intent gaze.

She got up from the couch, straightened her clothing, and pushed her hair away from her face. Since she'd arrived at the Tanners', she'd been French-braiding her hair, but it was always disheveled by the end of the day. As the children ran ahead of them to the kitchen, she said, "I know you said to put them to bed, but they begged so hard to wait up for you that I didn't have the heart to make them go. I hope you don't mind too much."

"Mind?" he said, laughing. "I was being considerate of you. You're supposed to have free evenings, and I didn't want you to be bothered with them, after you'd had them all day."

"I enjoyed the evening as much as they did. Besides, they needed help tonight, so I'm glad I was here. I'll tell you about it later."

He put his hand on her shoulder, and she darted a quick glance toward him. The expression in his blue eyes startled her, and she dropped her gaze quickly, not daring to interpret what she saw there. Impulsively, Mark embraced Alice in a brotherly hug, and for a moment, Alice rested her head on his shoulder.

Careful, Alice, don't misinterpret his caress—he's simply grateful to you for looking after his children, she told herself.

He dropped his arms, and she moved away from him casually, saying, "I can warm your dinner in the microwave if you haven't eaten."

"We had food sent in, so I've eaten, but the milk and muffins sound good."

"Did you have a difficult evening?" she asked as they walked companionably down the hallway to the kitchen.

He groaned. "We met with a rich *and* very difficult client—one of the officers had offended him, and he was threatening to withdraw all of his assets from the bank, so the CEO wanted all of us there to mollify him."

"Did it work?"

"Finally, but it was a long session." He yawned.

Kristin had already placed four glasses of milk on the table, and muffins on napkins for each of them. Alice had intended to go to her room and not infringe on this short time Mark had with his kids, but she knew Kristin wouldn't understand, so she sat down. She had no appetite, however, for as the children chattered about their day's activities, from time to time, she sensed Mark's eyes searching her face.

Mark took the last bite of his muffin and asked for another one. "Is it all right, Alice?" Kristin asked.

"Of course."

"Now, you kids, go upstairs, brush your teeth and get in bed. I'll be up to kiss you good-night as soon as I finish my snack," Mark said. "Kristin, help Eddie."

Alice started to tell him that Eddie didn't need any help, but she decided to let Mark find that out for himself.

As the sounds of their footsteps faded up the stairs, Mark spoke quietly, "What kind of help did they need tonight?"

"Do you realize that Kristin and Eddie are afraid you're going to die?"

His face blanched, and Alice continued, "They think they'll lose you like they did their mother. They can't understand why God let their mother die. I tried to talk with them and reassure them, but I don't know how to explain God's will to children. Betty said you're an excellent counselor—perhaps you can talk with them."

Mark laid down his fork, shoved the half-eaten muffin aside, and stared at the floor. At last he looked at her, and Alice was chilled by the bleak expression in his eyes.

"I can't give them any assurance when I don't have any for myself. I don't know what's going to happen to us."

He pushed back his chair, and without a word left the kitchen. His footsteps sounded leaden as he climbed the stairs.

Alice remembered something Betty once told her, "I think he's lost his faith, and that's a terrible thing to say about a man who was a powerhouse in the ministry." Alice had purposely watched to see if Betty's suspicions were true, but since Mark had always been upbeat, she decided that Betty was overly concerned. However, it had bothered Alice that God was never mentioned in the house, and that none of them attended church services. The family's spiritual life had been neglected during Clarice's illness, and Alice intended to start taking the children to Sunday school. But in light of Mark's words tonight, she suspected that he did have a serious problem.

If she was inadequate in comforting a couple of children, what words could she find to encourage Mark Tanner? And why should she concern herself about this man's happiness—she'd come here only to be a nanny to his children, hadn't she? Alice didn't dare truly answer that question—not even to herself.

Chapter Three

The next morning, Mark had reverted to his pleasant self, and Alice sometimes wondered if she'd dreamed that moment when he seemed defeated, as if life had handed him more trouble than he could handle. Yet she knew she hadn't imagined it, and during her daily devotions, she prayed for Mark's spiritual condition.

Mark had agreed to the housecleaning plan, and Alice had arranged for the women to come the day she took Kristin to church camp, for since Gran and Eddie were going along, the house would be empty for the workers. She'd replenished Kristin's wardrobe without Mark questioning the cost. He was impressed with the secondhand garments she'd purchased, not realizing that some of the items were new. He gave Kristin a ten-dollar bill for her camp expenses, and was none the wiser when Alice doubled the amount. For the first time since John Larkin had died and willed her a fortune, Alice felt good about her money.

Gran had protested when Alice invited her to go along.

"Oh, no, Alice, you don't want to be saddled with an old woman like me."

"Gran, you haven't been out of the house since I've been here, and that isn't healthy for you."

Interest dawning in her eyes, Gran continued to protest. "But I don't think I can get in that van of yours."

"My husband was in a wheelchair the last several months of his life, and the van is equipped with a lift, which will make it easy for you to get in."

"All right. It'll be nice to drive out in the country. The campsite is in a very pretty part of this state."

The camp was located near Charlottesville—the same camp Alice had attended when she was a girl, although quite a few improvements had been made since then, including an Olympic-size swimming pool. When she'd gone to camp, the swimming hole was in the creek, but she'd learned to swim there. It was at this camp that she'd dedicated her life to God, even then praying for a life of service. She'd thought her prayer had been fulfilled when she took care of John for several years, but perhaps that was just the beginning.

Since the round-trip drive would take several hours, Mark had hesitated to allow Eddie to go with them.

"He tires so easily," he said. "I'm sure that Ethel will be glad to keep him. She's helped out before when I didn't have anyone to stay with the children."

"But, Daddy, I want to see where Kristin is going."

With a worried look, Mark finally agreed, but Alice wondered if he'd had second thoughts, when just before they were ready to start, Ethel barged into the house.

"I'm taking care of Eddie while you're gone."

"Eddie is going with us," Kristin said. "Daddy said it's all right."

"Perhaps he changed his mind," Ethel said breezily, a smug look on her face as if she had information they didn't.

"I want to go, Alice," Eddie said.

"Of course, you're going, Eddie, unless Mark tells me differently within the next five minutes."

She turned to Gran, who was limping down the stairs, and reached out a hand to help her descend the last two steps.

"Then I'm coming with you, Alice," Ethel said. "You'll need help with Gran, and Eddie, as sickly as he is."

Eddie wilted at her statement, and annoyed, Alice said, "Eddie is *not* sickly. He doesn't need any help."

But short of physically removing Ethel from her car, Alice was helpless in the face of the woman's brashness, as Ethel took Gran's arm, led her out of the house, helped her into the van, and preempted the front seat where Alice had expected Kristin to sit. Her aggressive behavior was annoying, but since Ethel had been helpful during Clarice's illness and after her death, Alice wasn't in a position to antagonize a friend of the family. She was provoked at herself because part of her anger stemmed from Betty's comment that Ethel was angling for Mark's attention by befriending his children.

Ethel wasn't a bad-looking woman. She was of

medium height, with a slender waist, and shapely. Only a long thin nose kept her from having a beautiful face. Ethel was probably forty years of age, although she tried to disguise her few wrinkles with a heavy coat of makeup.

"Do you know how to find the camp?" she asked as Alice left the city behind and headed into open country.

"I attended camp there when I was a girl, but I wasn't sure how to get there from Richmond, so Mr. Tanner gave me directions."

"You called him 'Mark' earlier. Why change to Mr. Tanner now?"

"It depends on whom I'm talking to. I sometimes call him Daddy when I'm talking to his children."

That comment silenced Ethel for several miles, and when she started talking again, she addressed most of her remarks to Gran and the kids. Alice soon noted that Ethel had an adverse effect on Eddie. She constantly referred to his disability, and by the time they arrived at camp, Eddie was limp as a rag, and Alice had to persuade him to get out of the car.

"I don't feel good, Alice. I'll stay in the van."

"Nonsense! You need to walk around a bit, and we'll have lunch with Kristin before we start home."

They found a shady spot where Gran and Eddie could sit on a bench, and when Ethel would have taken control of Kristin's registration, Alice said firmly, "I'll go with Kristin to register and find out where she'll be staying. The rest of you stay here in the shade."

Picking up Kristin's suitcase, Alice headed toward a log building that had a registration sign tacked on a post.

The camp was located in a small river valley, with woodlands along its banks. A dozen log dormitories were scattered among the trees, and one long building with a wide veranda, that Alice took for the dining hall, was situated beside the swimming pool. A badminton court and a softball field were beyond the pool. From one point, they had a good view of the Blue Ridge Mountains.

Kristin placed a trembling hand on Alice's arm, and she knew that the child feared this new experience.

"I don't see Susie anywhere—she said she'd be here to meet me. She came to camp last year so she knows what to do."

"I'm sure she'll arrive soon, and we won't leave until she does come. I remember the first day I came to camp, and it was scary, but in a few hours, I felt right at home. You'll enjoy yourself."

"I'll miss Daddy."

"He'll miss you, too, but you'll be so busy with crafts, hiking and sports activities that the week will pass before you know it."

They entered the open door of the rustic building crowded with girls and their parents. One child detached herself from a group and ran toward Kristin.

"That's Susie," Kristin said in relief.

"Hi, Kristin. I've already registered and I was watching for you. We're assigned to Bear Cabin—it's a nice one. Come on, I'll show you what to do."

Alice placed the suitcase in a corner where a lot of other luggage was stacked, and queued up with the two girls to wait their turn at the registration table. A young woman joined them and, with a broad smile, said, "I'm Susie's mother, Erin Saberton. You must be Mrs. Larkin."

Alice shook hands with her. "Yes, I'm Kristin's nanny. I'm glad to meet you. I hope you'll let Susie visit Kristin when they return from camp. The house is too quiet."

With a laugh, Erin said, "It won't be quiet if Susie is visiting." She lowered her voice. "Susie's wanted to visit, but Mark has been so withdrawn since Clarice's death that I thought he didn't want visitors."

"He's gone so much that he does like to have evenings alone with his kids, but there's no reason Susie can't come during the daytime. I'll be glad to have her."

"When the Tanners had only part-time nannies, I hesitated to send another child for them to oversee. But thanks for your invitation—Susie will telephone before she comes."

It was almost noon by the time Kristin was settled in Bear Cabin—a small cottage with five sets of crude bunk beds. There were a couple of lavatories in the cabin, but a central bathhouse would take care of their other needs. Alice helped Kristin make up her bunk bed, which was right below Susie's. Mrs. Saberton had to return home, so Susie ate with Kristin and her family in the long dining room.

As he watched the campers, Eddie's spirits improved a little, showing interest in the place his sister would be living for a week. While they ate hot dogs, potato chips and cookies, Eddie said, "When can I come to camp, Alice?"

"Not until you're as old as Kristin."

"I doubt you'll be able to be a camper, Eddie, so I wouldn't count on it," Ethel said.

Eddie turned a piteous look in Alice's direction, and she patted him on the back. She was too angry to answer Ethel, but she had her emotions under control when they were driving back to Richmond. Gran settled down for a nap, and when Alice saw that Eddie was sleeping tight in his seat belt, head leaning forward, she said to Ethel, "Why do you persist in making an invalid out of Eddie? I talked with his pediatrician, and he said that Eddie's health problems have been corrected. He told me to encourage Eddie to live like any other five-year-old boy. I can't do that if you keep telling him he's sick."

Anger flashed from Ethel's black eyes. "I've been looking after Kristin and Eddie since their mother got sick. It's none of your business how I treat them."

"That's where you're wrong. Mark has hired me to look out for his children, and I'm going to do that to the best of my ability."

"But you're only a stranger—how can you know what's better for them than I do?"

"A stranger can often see things that others can't. For instance, Eddie has made a slave out of Kristin— she runs at his beck and call, and it isn't necessary. There isn't any reason he can't get a drink of water when he wants it, why he can't go up and down the stairs without help, and I hope to instill some independence in him this week. Gran isn't able to wait on him, I'm not going to, and I'll appreciate it if you don't interfere."

Ethel didn't respond, but the look she cast in Alice's direction was venomous, and Alice was convinced that she'd report the conversation to Mark.

The cleaning women were just finishing when Alice returned. Even from the outside, the house looked better because the windows were clean and shining, and the lemony fresh smell inside the house was stimulating. After she settled Gran and Eddie in their rooms for a nap, Alice went to the porch where the women were washing the paneling.

"The house looks great," she said. "It won't be so difficult to keep everything tidy now." When she paid them before they left, she tripled the amount that Mark had laid aside for them, and the woman to whom she gave the money, stared at her speculatively. Apparently this was more money then they usually received, and she hoped she hadn't overdone it. Since Mark was known to be hard up, people might start wondering where he was getting so much money.

The next night, Alice asked Mark to help her set up the computer, and he readily agreed. Since she wanted to supervise the children's use of the computer, they put it in her room.

Mark protested a little. "Maybe we'd better set this up in the dining room—you could still keep your eye on them when they're using the computer. They'll want to use it all the time, and you won't even have any privacy when you go to your room."

"We'll see how it goes first."

Since she knew Eddie would want to try it out at once, Alice had stopped by the video store and rented an educational game. While Mark played the game with Eddie, Alice sat in the rocker and picked up her sewing basket. She hadn't accomplished much on the tablecloth she was making for her sister since she'd come to the Tanners.

"Time for bed, Eddie," Mark said. "We'll get your shower, and I'll tuck you in."

Eddie went without much protest, and he came over to Alice, and kissed her cheek. "Thanks for bringing the computer, Alice. It's been a fun thing to do with Daddy."

Alice laid down her embroidery and hugged him tightly, shutting her eyes to keep any tears from escaping. "You're a good boy, Eddie," she said. "I'm glad you've had a nice time."

"I'll come back down after Eddie's in bed, Alice. I noticed you have a Scrabble game on the hard drive. Can I challenge you to a game?"

"But, Daddy, I'm afraid to go upstairs without Kristin. Won't you stay upstairs with me?"

Mark hesitated, but he said, "Not tonight, Son. You'll soon be asleep, and I'll hear you if you call."

Alice had always enjoyed playing Scrabble, and had been good at it, but she was no match for Mark. She could readily understand Betty's comments about his superior intelligence, for he quickly spelled out a word clue. They played two games, and Mark won both of them. But Alice excused herself, for she couldn't concentrate on the game, finding it difficult to think of any words. Mark's name rolled over and over in her mind excluding all others, and of course, in Scrabble, she wasn't allowed to use given names. They sat close together to have a good view of the screen, and when their shoulders touched or hands collided as they typed in their answers, Alice's pulse raced and her temperature soared.

"That's not very nice of you—beating me on my own computer," she said when Mark pushed back his chair. "I'll have to withdraw your computer privileges."

Mark's eyes softened into a smile. "Oh, don't do

that. This is the most pleasant evening I've spent for ages. We may do this every night.''

"Not if you keep beating me,'' she retorted, a smile on her face.

Mark stood up and stretched, and Alice looked away quickly. "I'll check to see if Eddie is okay, and then let's sit on the patio. It's a pleasant evening. I'll open the window in Eddie's room, so we'll hear him if he calls.''

Don't do it, Alice. Keep this relationship on a professional level.

But despite her qualms, when Mark came downstairs, she went with him to the backyard. He cleaned the lounge chairs with a cloth, and when she was seated, he stretched out on the chair beside her, breathing deeply.

"Wow! It's good to relax. I didn't even take time for lunch today at the office, and thank you for the good meal tonight. After fasting all day, I really enjoyed it. You're a good cook, Alice. You must have had lots of experience.''

"My mother taught me and my sister to cook when we were girls, and I did several 4-H projects on foods and nutrition, so I started at an early age.'' She didn't mention that after her marriage, they'd kept the same cook John had employed when he was a widower.

"Besides the work at the bank, the care of the kids almost overwhelms me at time. I had no idea the kind of burden a single parent carries, and sometimes I blush in shame when I realize how blithely I used to counsel single parents.''

"But you're a good father, Mark—you've done well with your children.''

She saw him shake his head in the semidarkness, and a lock of hair fell over his forehead. "No, I'm not really. I'm neglecting some of the most important things they need to know."

She wondered if he referred to his lack of spiritual training. They were sitting close enough that Alice could have reached out and touched his arm in encouragement, but she refrained.

"It takes time, Mark. It's only been six months."

"I keep telling myself that, and months before Clarice's death, she wasn't able to deal with the children's problems. I shielded her as much as possible." He sighed. "But I don't find it as overwhelming as I did a few months ago. It's taking time to deal with my hang-ups, but I'm working on it." He took a deep breath. "Thanks for listening to me, Alice. I'm probably imposing on you, but it's been a long since I've had an adult to listen to me. A minister needs someone at home to support him, because he's usually giving of himself all day. Even though I'm not working with a church congregation as I used to do, I'm a counselor at the bank, and I still have to deal with other people's problems."

"When are you intending to take another church?" Alice dared to ask.

"I don't know, Alice—I really don't know what to do."

The rest of the week, as soon as Eddie was settled in, it seemed natural for Mark and Alice to seek the peace and comfort of the patio. Alice excused her actions by believing it was a good time to discuss her rehab program for Eddie and to talk of Kristin's maturation, but she knew those weren't the only reasons she wanted to be in Mark's company. Sometimes they didn't talk much, but Alice felt that the times of silence were good for him. After being with people all day, he didn't need to talk—he only needed a companion.

And her work with Eddie had resulted in some progress. After one day of whining, Eddie learned to do a few things for himself. He walked slowly up and down stairs by himself, he went to the bathroom unattended, and Alice showed him how to straighten his bedsheets and cover them with a spread. Every morning, after he'd eaten his breakfast, she walked with him around the neighborhood streets, increasing the distance each day.

When he dozed over his food one night at dinner, Mark gazed at him in concern, but he offered no complaint to Alice.

Parents were invited to the closing exercises at the camp on Friday evening, and Mark arranged to leave work a few hours early on that day to attend.

"I'd like for you to go with me, Alice, unless you have other plans for tonight," Mark had said as he picked up his briefcase that morning and started to work.

This isn't wise, Alice cautioned herself mentally, but she heard herself saying, "I'll be happy to go— I'm eager to find out how Kristin enjoyed herself." She had a giddy sense of excitement as she helped Eddie dress, and later as she looked in the closet to choose her own garments. She'd mostly worn jeans and sweatshirts since she'd come to Richmond, but she chose a white cotton knit skirt styled with a self-sash, a multistitched elasticized waist, and inseam pockets. She pulled a blouse of cream fabric with an overall floral pattern over her head. Her long blond hair was brushed backward, and secured with a barrette. She strapped on a pair of white leather sandals and thought she looked well-groomed for a trip to camp.

Alice prepared dinner early, and she ate with Gran and Eddie before Mark came home. She wrapped a plate of food with foil and kept it warm for him in the oven.

"Oh, you didn't need to do that, Alice," Mark protested. "I often miss a meal."

"Which you shouldn't," she said. "Take time to eat, while I put the dishes and pans in the dishwasher." She was sure Mark had gained a few pounds, and she wanted to continue the trend until he looked more like the man in the picture she often looked at on the living room mantel.

He laid his briefcase and coat aside, washed his hands in the utility room, and sat down at the table.

"I'm imposing on you, Alice, and I shouldn't do it, but I make so many decisions that it's occasionally nice for someone to just tell me what to do."

By now, Alice had learned Mark's dietary habits. She took a salad from the refrigerator and placed it before him with a bottle of Italian dressing. She poured chilled tea over a glass of ice cubes and dropped in a sliver of lemon. When he finished with the salad, she handed him the warm plate of baked turkey, potato cakes and green peas.

"I didn't prepare dessert, for I think they'll serve ice cream to everybody at the camp."

Mark didn't voice any further appreciation, but it was reward enough for Alice to see him enjoying his meal while he looked over the front page of the newspaper that she'd laid by his plate.

While she secured Eddie in the back seat of Mark's station wagon, Alice suppressed a sense of excitement, reminding herself that she wasn't a girl going on a first date. She was a nanny now, and her role was to look after Mark Tanner's children, not fancy that he'd invited her because he wanted her company; but she had trouble remembering that when she listened to Mark, who was an engaging conversationalist.

"This reminds me of old times," he said, as they left Richmond on I-64. "I used to direct a camp every summer, usually for boys in their early teens. It was a rewarding experience, and I've missed it."

"I often camped when I was a girl. We lived on a farm, and I went to 4-H camps more often than to church camps, and I loved them."

"What about family, Alice? Do you still have your parents?"

"Yes, they live in a retirement community now, but the farm is still in the family, and my aunt and uncle are the tenants. I have a sister, too, who's divorced with two children, so I have some understanding of what's it's like to be a single parent."

"My parents live in Tennessee," Mark said, "and we don't see them often. They own a business in a small town, and they can't get away very often. They were here six months ago for the—" he paused and looked over his shoulder at Eddie "—the funeral," he continued. "They feel badly that they aren't close enough to help out with the kids, and I did consider moving back to my hometown, so I could have some help. But I have to stay in a metropolitan area to make the money I need right now."

Seeing that Eddie was getting fidgety, Alice said, "Let's play a game, Eddie."

"We can't play a game in the car."

"Oh, it's a travel game. You count the number of animals you see in the fields on the left-hand side of the road, and I'll count the ones I see on my side. We'll get a point for each animal. How far can you count?"

"I can count up to twenty. Kristin taught me."

"Then, as long as there aren't more than twenty in any field, you have it made."

Alice fished a small notebook out of her purse. "I'll keep score."

Mark entered into the spirit of the game, and since Eddie was too short to see what they were approaching, he would call out, "Coming up on the left—look quickly."

"Hey!" Alice protested in mock reproof after a few miles. "Two against one isn't fair."

"Oh, stop complaining," Mark said. "Coming up on the right—a large herd of cattle. Start counting."

Laughing, Alice counted, "One, two, three..." By the time they reached the camp, she and Eddie were neck and neck in total points. As he drove into the parking lot, Mark said, "I don't know why I haven't thought of something like that. Eddie has never been a good traveler."

"Most children aren't, I understand," she answered. "He didn't enjoy his trip to the camp on Monday."

"No, Ethel said he was listless."

Well, thanks, Ethel. Apparently she'd reported everything to Mark. Alice wasn't aware that she contacted him in the evening, so she must have telephoned him at the bank.

Kristin and Susie raced to meet them when they approached the council circle where the closing program was to be held. One look at Kristin's tanned face and the delight that flamed from her blue eyes repaid Alice for the money she'd spent on the child. *If only she had the right to give this family everything they needed!*

Mark knelt and took Kristin in his arms. "Well, honey, have you had a good time?"

"Yes, Daddy, and I want to come back next year. We've been horseback riding, swimming and hiking. But the food hasn't been very good." She turned to Alice. "I've missed your good meals. If it hadn't been for the snacks I bought, I'd have gone to bed hungry every night." Worry crossed her face. "I've spent almost all of that twenty dollars you gave me."

From his kneeling position, Mark flashed a quick look toward Alice, and in spite of herself, her face grew warm.

"I want to ride horses, too," Eddie said. "Why can't I come to camp?"

"You're too little, Eddie," his sister said bossily. "But there is a family camp—we could come as a family sometime," she said hopefully.

"We'll plan on that for next year," Mark said, as he stood up.

"Hey, Brother Tanner," a man's voice sounded, and soon Mark was surrounded by several men—some embraced him, others thumped him on the shoulder. "We've missed seeing you at our ministerial meetings."

It occurred to Alice that these men had known Mark when he was serving at Tyler Memorial Church. As they continued toward the campfire burning in the distance, one older man, whom Mark had introduced as "Reverend Astor, my friend and mentor," walked beside Mark, who was leading Eddie. Alice moved forward to join Susie and Kristin, as both of them talked at the same time about the incidents they'd enjoyed during the week. Although she didn't intend to eavesdrop, she couldn't avoid hearing the conversation behind her.

"Brother Mark," the man said, "it's a great disappointment to me that you've forsaken the ministry. Have you forgotten the promise you made to serve our Lord with your life? Surely you aren't happy rejecting your divine calling."

Mark didn't answer at first, and Alice envisioned wrinkles creasing his brow, the bleak look in his eyes and a rigid cast on his lips—expressions she'd noticed a few times when he didn't think anyone was looking.

"You know why I had to resign from the pastorate. My wife was dying, and at that point, I believed my priority was my family, rather than my church."

"I agree with that, and it was noble of you to sacrifice your career for your family. But what about now? I've had several churches inquire about you and would willingly call you to become their leader."

"I've had churches contact me, but not one of them can come close to paying me the salary I'm receiving at the bank. And I'm not being mercenary—I've never demanded anything from a church—but my debts have accumulated to such an extent that if I don't pay them, I'll have to declare bankruptcy and end up losing our home.''

"It's obvious to me, Mark, that you're placing your trust in the wrong security. You've been a pastor long enough to know that God meets the needs of His people. Trust Him for the future, not the security of a large salary.''

Bitterly, Mark said, "I trusted Him for everything, but when He forgot Mark Tanner and his family, I had to turn elsewhere.''

Over the girls' chatter, Alice heard an audible moan from Reverend Astor. "If I hadn't heard it from your own mouth, I wouldn't believe you made that statement. Don't let your troubles overwhelm you.''

"I'm sorry," Mark said, "I don't know why I said such a thing—I really don't believe it. It's just that I'm having trouble coping with my own life right now, and I don't believe I'm capable of dealing with the needs of a church congregation.''

Reverend Astor put his arms around Mark's shoulders. "I know you've had a difficult time, Mark, but you'll come out of it a better man. Remember Job's example. He had a lot of trouble, but he kept his faith in God's goodness through it all.''

"My friend, I've read the book of Job so much in the last two years that those pages in my Bible are almost threadbare. There's hardly a day, I haven't voiced Job's words, "But he knoweth the way that I take: when he has tried me, I shall come forth as gold.''

"God bless you, Mark," Reverend Astor said. "I'll continue to keep you in my prayers.''

When Mark again walked by Alice's side, in a low

voice, he said, "I suppose you heard the raking over the coals I just had."

Alice nodded. "I couldn't keep from hearing. I'm sorry, Mark—try to forget it. Be happy for Kristin tonight."

"I can't forget it. I know I'm not fulfilling God's will for my life, and it's making me miserable."

His eyes mirrored the anguish reflected in his words, and in spite of herself, Alice lifted a hand and touched his cheek. "One of my grandfather's favorite sayings was, 'The sky is the darkest just before the dawn.' Dawn will come for you before long."

He reached out and squeezed her hand as she lowered it from his face. "The darkness has lifted a lot in the past three weeks," he said meaningfully.

On their way home from the camp, Mark was unusually quiet. Alice chose to sit in the back seat to give Kristin an opportunity to talk to her father, but eventually both Eddie and Kristin went to sleep. Alice made no effort to engage Mark in conversation, for she suspected he was wrestling with God much as Jacob in the Old Testament had done when he ran away from his brother's wrath. If Mark Tanner had been the powerful voice for God that so many people believed he was, then God wasn't going to release this man from the vows of service he'd taken without a mighty struggle. While Mark struggled, Alice prayed that God would once again bring peace to Mark's heart, inspire him to accept a renewed call to ministry, and that his financial burden would be eased.

Alice believed that God often expected an individual to put wings to her own prayers. Only God could help Mark with his spiritual needs, but she had the means to alleviate Mark's financial burden. *Was it the right thing to do?* She couldn't decide.

When Mark turned into his driveway, Kristin stirred as the garage door lifted and the light came on, but Eddie still slept soundly. Mark cast a fond look at his son. "Don't waken him," he said. "I'll carry him upstairs and put him to bed."

"I'll take care of Kristin."

Later, they met in the upstairs hallway after the children were in bed.

"It seems we have a little matter of ten dollars to discuss," he said, but his light tone indicated he wasn't angry about it.

"There isn't anything to discuss. I have an income from my late husband, and it didn't hurt me to help Kristin. I've been to camp, and I know how fast spending money disappears." He paused at his bedroom, his hand on the door, and she said, "I'll see you in the morning."

"Good night, Alice. I enjoyed your company this evening."

She didn't answer—she couldn't.

"I'm going to church this morning," Alice announced as the Tanners enjoyed a leisurely breakfast on Sunday. "Anyone interested in going with me?"

"I want to go," Kristin said. "They taught us in camp that if we don't go to church, we forget the important things in life."

"I'm planning on going to Tyler Memorial—that's where my friend Betty attends."

"That's where I want to go," Kristin said excitedly. "It's Susie's church. Daddy, why don't you go with us?"

"Not today, honey. Eddie is still tired from his trip to camp."

Determined not to pressure Mark and allow the Holy Spirit to do His work in Mark's heart, Alice turned to Gran. "What about you?"

"I don't know," she said hesitantly. "I'm pretty slow getting in and out of the car."

"Then we'll start early and attend the second service. Kristin will be in Sunday school while we're at worship." She turned to Mark. "If we allow a half hour, will that be enough time?"

"Yes, I should think so." He was busily buttering his toast and wouldn't look at her.

"All right, everybody who wants to go to church, be ready in an hour."

"I want to go, too," Eddie said.

Mark looked at Alice then. "Do you want to bother with him? This is supposed to be your day off."

"*Everybody* was included in my invitation. Besides, he isn't any bother. I know this is your day with the children, but they should be in Sunday school. I'll take the rest of the day off. I'm going swimming with Betty and her family this afternoon."

Betty smiled broadly when she met Alice and her adopted family at the door of the church, and Alice frowned at her as she assisted Gran up the ramp constructed to the right of the steps.

"Can you find your class, Kristin, and will you take Eddie to his?"

"Yes. Come on, Eddie." She grabbed her brother

by the hand and hustled him down the sidewalk to the large educational unit adjacent to the church.

An usher took Gran's arm and assisted her to one of the front pews where facilities were available for worshipers with hearing aids. "I'll sit with Betty, Gran—see you after worship."

The organist's prelude mounted in crescendo, and under cover of the loud music, Betty said, "Couldn't get Mark to come, huh?"

"I didn't ask him directly, but I do think his conscience bothered him when the rest of us left."

"I hope so," Betty answered. "When I think of some of the sermons he preached to us on commitment, and made us feel lower than snakes because we weren't living up to our Christian potential, I long to have him squirm under the messages this minister is preaching. T'would do him good."

Although Alice agreed with Betty to some extent, she didn't want to hear Mark criticized. "He's still hurting. We should pray for him, not find fault with him."

Betty lifted her eyebrows, smiled broadly, and said, as the organist brought the prelude to a loud and reverberating conclusion, "Well! You *have* fallen in a big way!"

Alice flushed. "It's your fault—you shouldn't have sent me there."

Throughout the worship service, Alice sensed Betty's amusement and heard her faint chuckles. It was annoying, and Alice had a half notion not to go swimming with her in the afternoon.

Monday morning, the phone rang, with a man asking for Mark. When Alice told him that Mark was at work, he said, "Will you give him a message? I'm the financial administrator at the hospital, and we've learned that the insurance company will not pay anything on several of the statements we submitted for his wife's treatments."

"Her death occurred months ago. Isn't that a long time for a decision?"

"Well, yes," he said, "but I submitted the statements a second time, hoping they'd pay something. I'll mail the bills to Mr. Tanner, but I wanted him to know in advance."

"How much do the bills total?" Alice asked, knowing well enough that she was interfering in something that wasn't her business.

"About eight thousand," he said.

Poor Mark!

Mark seemed more weary than usual when he came home, and Alice put off telling him about the telephone message until Kristin and Eddie went to bed. She'd gone upstairs to check on the children, to be sure they were all right, and when she came downstairs, Mark sat in his office. His checkbook was open on the desk before him, and he was sorting through the day's mail.

She paused on the threshold, and he gave her an encouraging smile. Her expression must have warned him, for the smile faded, and he said, "Is something wrong with Eddie?"

She shook her head. "The kids are fine, but I did have a disturbing telephone call today." She couldn't look at him as she told him the bad news. When she finished and glanced in his direction, his head was lowered to his hands.

"And I thought I was making some headway out

of this mess," he mumbled. "Alice, I don't know what I'm going to do."

Alice was of the opinion that he could cope with the situation better if he wasn't out of fellowship with God, but this was no time for a sermon. The man needed compassion now, and without stopping to think of the consequences, she rounded the desk, put an arm around his shoulders and massaged the tense muscles in his neck. "Remember the night is always darkest before the dawn," she whispered. "You're a strong man, and you're going to overcome these problems."

He moved to put his arm around her waist and draw her closer, but Alice gently released him.

"I'll be back in a few minutes," she promised, as with misty eyes, she left the room and hurried to the kitchen. When she returned, she brought a steaming cup of tea. He still sat with his head in his hands.

She didn't touch him again, but she set the cup on the desk in front of him, saying softly, "I realize this is something you have to work out alone, but I want you to know that I hurt with you."

Alice went to bed, but not to sleep, for she couldn't relax until about two o'clock when she heard him leave his office and slowly climb the stairs to his bedroom. What could she do to help him?

"Hello, Alice," the cheery voice said when she answered the phone the next day. "This is Erin Saberton. Susie wants to come and play with Kristin this afternoon, and I have a boy about Eddie's age. Are you up to having four kids in the house for a few hours?"

"Sure, if you'll come along and help referee," Alice said with a laugh. "We can have a cup of coffee while the children play."

"I was hoping you'd ask. We'll be there at two o'clock."

When they arrived, the children went into the family room to watch cartoons, and Alice took Erin to the kitchen.

"You can't imagine how happy I am to see this household back to some sense of normalcy. You've performed a miracle in a few weeks, Alice. I don't know how you've done it."

"With a lot of prayer and patience," Alice said, laughing, as she poured a cup of coffee for each of them and put a plate of banana nut bread on the table. "It hasn't been easy to be in a home with so many people, for I've lived alone for over a year."

"You're a widow, I understand."

Alice nodded. "But I feel that it's right for me to be here, and I believe I am making a difference. You know Betty St. Claire, don't you?"

"Yes, we're friends."

"She's the one who asked me to take this on, and when she told me the need, I felt God calling me to do what I could."

Erin nibbled on the banana bread and complimented Alice on her cooking abilities. "I assume you don't need to work."

"That's true, but I'd appreciate it if you don't noise that around."

Erin laughed. "Gotcha," she said, and she lowered her voice. "Mark has needed someone to give him a helping hand for years, and I mean, even before his wife got sick. I know we're not supposed to speak ill of the dead, but Clarice was never the kind of wife he needed. She was completely self-centered, resented the time he spent with his parishioners, and expected him to assume more than his share of home responsibilities.''

Alice's face flushed, and she said, ''I had no idea! Betty didn't say anything, and I assumed that all was well here before Clarice's illness.''

Erin shook her head. ''Mark is such a giving person—as a pastor, there was never any request too insignificant for him to give his full attention. So when he came home, he needed a wife to love and pamper him, not one who acted like a martyr because he'd been out all day doing his job.''

Alice didn't want to hear anymore, and she was glad when Kristin stuck her head in the kitchen door and said, ''We're bored. What can we do?''

Alice stood and cleared the dishes from the table. ''It's too nice a day to spend indoors. Why don't we all go outside? If you're up to it, Erin, we might play softball with the kids. I found a ball and bat in one of the closets.''

''Probably the ones that Mark used when he coached our Little League team at the church.''

Erin's son, Troy, was boisterous and loud, and he intimidated Eddie, who hesitated to leave the house.

''I don't know how to play ball,'' he said, reverting to his whiny voice that Alice hadn't heard for a couple of weeks.

''We'll show you,'' Troy said. He grabbed Eddie's hand. ''Come on.''

Eddie pulled back, but Alice said, ''This will be fun, Eddie.''

''I want to ride horses, not play ball.''

An idea had been forming in Alice's mind about

his fixation on horses, but she couldn't do anything about that this afternoon. Alice lifted Eddie, carried him down the steps, and set him on the ground.

Shortly, they had a game underway with Erin playing on the side of the Tanners, and Alice paired with Susie and Troy. Although timid at first, Eddie soon began to enjoy the game, until Troy hit a ball with a lot of power. The ball went straight toward Eddie, who stared at the ball, mesmerized. He didn't move, and it hit him in the stomach—hard. Eddie toppled over like a felled tree.

Alice ran to Eddie, her heart thumping big time. "Is he dead, Alice?" Kristin screamed, and at that inopportune time, Ethel Pennington walked into the backyard.

"What's going on here?"

Alice ignored her as she checked Eddie's pounding pulse, but it wasn't more rapid than was normal for the activity he'd experienced.

"What's going on here?" Ethel repeated, and Kristin answered.

"Alice made Eddie play ball, and he got hit in the belly. He might be dead."

Ethel tried to crowd in through the excited children, but Erin outmaneuvered her and knelt on the other side of Eddie, who was already stirring.

"He had the breath knocked out of him," Erin said.

"That's all."

"That's all!" Ethel said shrilly. "He's such a delicate child—he could have been killed."

Eddie's face was white when Alice helped him to his feet. Looking from one to the other of the concerned faces around him, he wheezed, "What happened?"

"The ball hit you in the belly," Troy shouted, "and knocked the wind out of you. I didn't know you were such a sissy, or I wouldn't have hit the ball so hard."

"Hush, Troy," his mother said.

"You come with me, Eddie," Ethel said, taking his arm. "I'm going to put you to bed."

Alice slumped down in one of the lawn chairs, and didn't make any effort to resist Ethel. "There's some banana bread and lemonade ready in the kitchen, Kristin. You serve some to your friends. Erin and I will be in soon."

"Don't let this bother you, Alice. No harm was done," Erin said. "It isn't unusual for children to be hurt when they're playing."

"I shouldn't have insisted that he play, but the doctor told me that he'd been pampered too much, and that Eddie should live like any other boy. That's all I was trying to do. I can't imagine Mark's reaction."

"Perhaps he won't know about it."

"With two kids involved, to say nothing of Ethel, whom I'm convinced reports to Mark on everything I do! He'll hear about it."

The Sabertons and Ethel left about the same time, and Alice went to check on Eddie. He was in bed, and Kristin was reading to him. Alice sat down on the edge of his bed.

"Tummy sore?" she asked, as she gently lifted the blanket and ran her hand over his stomach. She couldn't see a bruise of any kind.

"Just a little," Eddie said, "but Ethel said I'd

have to stay in bed. I wanted to play some more and show Troy Saberton that I'm not a sissy.''

Alice lifted Eddie and cradled him in her arms. ''Of course, you aren't a sissy. That could have happened to any of us. Troy didn't mean to hurt you. You rest until dinner is ready, and you can get up then.''

At that inauspicious moment, Mark bolted into the room.

''Daddy, you're home early,'' Kristin said.

He didn't answer her, but rushed over to Eddie. ''Are you all right, Son?'' He ignored Alice, and she gave him her place on the bed and left the room.

She stood at the sink peeling potatoes when he entered the kitchen fifteen minutes later. She supposed he'd gotten the whole story from the children—hopefully they'd described the situation more correctly than Ethel would have done. Alice turned to face him, and he was angry—she'd seen him disillusioned, discouraged and downhearted, but she hadn't seen him angry until this moment. His blue eyes flashed like steel, and his lips trembled.

''I told you to take it easy with him. I hadn't paid much attention before when Ethel told me you were pushing Eddie to try things he shouldn't do.''

She resented being put on the defensive, and she spoke more harshly than she would normally have done. ''And his doctor told me that Eddie has been pampered too long and that he should be treated like any other boy. Every time Ethel comes here, she undermines any progress he's made by telling him he's sick.''

Alice was so disappointed that Mark had chosen to believe Ethel rather than her, that her normally low voice was shrill when she continued, "If you want Ethel to take care of your children, that's your decision, but if I stay, she has to stop interfering."

"I usually don't pay much attention to Ethel, but it's obvious that Eddie could have been hurt badly today. What if that ball had hit him in the head?"

"I'm terribly sorry that Eddie was hurt, but if he lives a normal life, he's bound to have these accidents. Have you forgotten what it's like to be a boy? If he doesn't get out of that room and learn to play with other children, he's always going to be a recluse."

"He's my child—don't you think I can make the right decisions for him?"

Alice wanted to tell him that he hadn't made the right decision when he stopped taking his children to Sunday school, but this wasn't the time to bring up that subject.

"In three days, I will have been here a month when we were to determine if I was suited for this position, but it isn't too early to make the decision now. Perhaps I have overstepped my authority, but I only did what I thought was best for Eddie, while at the same time trying to lift the burden you're carrying. If you can't see that Kristin and Eddie are happier, better adjusted children than they were when I came, I *want* to leave. I'm going to finish dinner now, but before the evening's over, I want to know your decision."

Ignoring the stricken look in his eyes at her words, she turned her back and tried to peel potatoes with hands that trembled. The blood pounded so loudly in her head that she couldn't hear, so she felt his presence behind her before she heard his steps. Mark placed his hands on her shoulders, and the paring knife clattered to the sink top. He turned her gently to face him.

"I don't want you to leave, Alice," he said softly, and her eyes locked with his.

"Why?" she whispered.

He slowly shook his head, and she couldn't tell if he didn't know why he didn't want her to leave, or that he wouldn't tell her.

"Will you stay?" His voice was soft and intimate.

She couldn't speak, but she lifted her hand, caressed the dimple on his cheek, knowing within her heart that his reason for asking her to stay was the same reason that made it impossible for her to leave.

Chapter Four

Dinner was a silent affair, even though Eddie ate a good meal, obviously none the worse for his accident. In fact, he seemed somewhat proud of the fact that he'd been knocked out. All of the family must have sensed the tension between Mark and Alice, and she noticed Kristin looking from one to the other with anxiety. It took so little to upset the security of these children. Mark made an effort to keep a conversation going, but Alice couldn't have spoken if she'd wanted to. Mark had asked her to stay, but she hadn't promised. *What should she do?*

Mark took the children into the living room when they'd finished eating, and Gran helped Alice remove the dishes from the table. After the dishwasher was filled, and Alice was washing the pans, Gran said, "Don't be upset, Alice. Eddie isn't hurt."

"I'm thankful for that, but I'm sorry it happened."

"Mark won't be angry for long," Gran assured Alice.

Alice hugged the stooped shoulders. "Thanks,

Gran. It's comforting to know that I have you on my side. I hope you have a good rest tonight.''

As Gran guided her walker toward the stairs, Alice went into her room and shut the door. What had Mark meant by his words? she wondered. Probably she was no more to him than a shoulder to cry on or a listening ear, but if Mark was learning to care for her, that would complicate their situation. If his feelings for her compared to her love for him, she'd have to leave, for it wouldn't be long before others would notice their mutual attraction. If only a month in his home had this effect on her, she'd be risking her reputation and his if she continued to stay. Already, she was willing to take this man and his family for her own. At her age, she should have known better.

Alice didn't turn on a light, but sat in the rocking chair and stared out the window, observing as twilight faded to darkness, listening to a cardinal's clear tones as it heralded the end of the day. To achieve some comfort, she took off her sandals and unbraided her hair to let it hang loosely around her shoulders. Slowly, she rocked back and forth, trying not to think, but in her mind, she reviewed every minute she'd spent in this home.

So deep was her concentration that she jumped when a knock sounded on the door. She padded across the floor in her bare feet and paused momentarily with her hand on the doorknob before she turned it.

Mark peered into the darkness. ''Were you asleep? I didn't know you'd turned off the light.''

''No, I wasn't asleep. I've been trying to sort things out in my mind.''

''Will you come into the office? We need to talk.''

She moved past him and down the hallway to his office. She perched on the edge of the chair she'd occupied the first day she came to this house and Mark took his chair behind the desk.

"I want to apologize," he said, "for...for several things, but right now, for losing my temper with you. I know you can't understand why I'm so protective of Eddie, but you only see him as he is now, a reasonably healthy child." He swiveled around in his chair and took a family portrait from a bookshelf.

"That's the last picture we have of our family before Clarice became ill. See how Eddie looked then."

Alice couldn't bring herself to look at Mark standing beside his wife, so she focused on Eddie—a frail child—whom Mark held in his arms.

"That's the way I think of Eddie—spiritless, a bluish tinge to his skin, not able to walk more than a few feet before he gasped for breath. I can't count the nights I've sat by his bed wondering if he'd live until morning."

"Please, Mark, you don't have to explain. I'm the one who should apologize. I overstepped myself, but I want you to know that I was doing only what I thought was good for your kids. I've always wanted children of my own, and I suppose I took my maternal frustrations out on your family."

"And as for the other apology I should make..."

Alice held up her hand. "It's better to leave some things unsaid. I don't want any more apologies."

"Perhaps you're right, but without referring to what happened in the kitchen this evening, I must say something."

He stood up and leaned against the desk close to Alice, but he didn't look directly at her. "I don't have any plans to remarry—you know what a financial bind I'm in, my two children have to take first priority, and I'm not where I should be spiritually. There's not a day that I don't wrestle with my decision to return to the ministry. I don't have anything to offer a wife.''

Except yourself, she thought dismally. She reached out and laid a hand on his arm. ''I understand, Mark, so please don't say anything else.''

He squeezed her hand slightly and resumed his seat at the desk.

''But you will stay with us?''

''Yes, for the time being at least, but I'll be honest—I'm not sure it's wise. It may be a mistake for us and the children.''

''We'll risk it. Even after only a month, I don't see how we could manage without you.''

It was easier to talk about her role as a nanny if one didn't look into Mark's eyes and read the message they conveyed. ''I'm willing to continue with the status quo. I'll need to go to Alexandria occasionally, but we can work that out without any problem.''

''You can set your own hours, but I *must* pay you the accepted wage for a nanny. The situation would be impossible otherwise.''

''I'll ask Betty what it is.'' He needed the money more than she did, but now wasn't the time to mention her financial status. She'd use what money he paid her for his family—perhaps start a college fund for Eddie and Kristin.

''Since we have that settled, I want to discuss something else with you. If you approve, I want to take Gran and the children to our family farm for a week. For some reason, Eddie is interested in horses, and there's a pony at the farm he can ride. If his interest persists, there are probably riding stables near Richmond where he can ride occasionally.''

''I'm sure there are. You say it's your family's farm?''

''My grandfather bought it, and it passed along to my father.'' She withheld the information that the farm belonged to her now, for John had bought the property to enable her parents to have enough money to move into the retirement community.

''Gran isn't your responsibility. You don't have to plan for her—she can stay here, especially when I'm home at night.''

''She might like a change. The house is a rambling frame structure with four rooms upstairs, and a bedroom downstairs. As I mentioned before my aunt and uncle, Margaret and Landon Wilcox, are the tenants, and they sleep downstairs, but they won't mind turning their bed over to Gran.''

''It'll be awfully quiet around here with all of you gone,'' he said with a slight smile.

''You're welcome to come, too.''

''Maybe over the weekend. When do you plan to go?''

''Week after next, if everybody agrees. I'll have to telephone Aunt Margaret to see if our visit is convenient for her, but perhaps you'd better clear it with the kids first. I'll talk to Gran about it.''

''I'll discuss the trip with Kristin and Eddie tomorrow night, but I'm sure they'll be enthusiastic. Kristin had such a good time at camp, and if I mention horses, Eddie will want to go.''

Alice eased out of the chair. ''Perhaps you'd better

say 'pony,' since there aren't any horses on the farm. My sister's children learned to ride on the pony, and he'll be safe enough for Eddie.''

Mark moved close to her—too close for her comfort. ''I can't believe the change you've made in our home in a month's time. Maybe you're a guardian angel sent to help us,'' he said lightly, with an amused look in his eyes. ''With that blond hair tumbling over your shoulders, you're so beautiful that you even look like a proverbial angel. My life is still messed up, but it's more bearable now that you're here.''

He gently drew her into a tight embrace, and with his lips close to hers, he whispered, ''I couldn't answer the question you asked me earlier about why I wanted you to stay here.'' He covered her lips with his, stifling Alice's soft gasp.

We can't let this happen, she thought, but it was her mind speaking, not her heart. It would be easier to stop the ocean's tides than to prevent the love they shared.

''Now you know,'' Mark said, as she trembled in his embrace. ''Just this once. Tomorrow morning, you'll be the nanny in the house, and I'll be your employer.''

Her arms lingered around his neck, and she brushed her lips softly across the dimple on his cheek. ''It won't be that simple, but I'll do my best to make it work.''

Alice was still in the kitchen the following night preparing for the next day's breakfast when she heard Kristin and Eddie running down the hallway.

''We want to go, Alice,'' Kristin said excitedly,

and Eddie latched on to Alice's legs. Mark followed the children into the kitchen.

"I assume you've told them," she said, and her eyes sparkled.

"Plenty of enthusiasm about visiting the farm, so make your plans. One of our friends lives on a farm, and they've visited there a few times."

"It's getting hot here in the city now," Alice said, "so it'll be a welcome relief for all of us to be in a rural area, and when we return, we can go to the pool some afternoons."

"I learned to swim at camp, but Eddie can't."

"He'll be able to swim by the end of summer," Alice promised.

Mark protested, "Well, I don't know...."

"It will be all right, Mark. I'll watch him carefully. I'll telephone tomorrow and make the arrangements. If it's all right with Margaret and Landon, we'll go next Monday."

Although the children were enthusiastic, Gran absolutely refused to go with them.

"I appreciate the invitation, Alice, but going to a farm is no treat for me. I grew up in the country when times were hard, and I don't have any fond memories of my childhood."

"But I don't like to leave you here alone."

"I can manage quite well, and Mark might be lonely coming home to an empty house. I'll be able to prepare some food to help him."

"He may join us over the weekend."

"That's fine, and I'm happy you're taking the children, but a farm is no place for me. I can't walk well enough to travel over uneven ground, and I'm better off where I am. Believe me, you'll all have a better time if I stay in Richmond.''

When Ethel heard about their trip to the farm, she volunteered at once. "I'll come in and help you prepare dinner each night, Gran Watson. We don't want Mark to be lonely.''

Ethel cast a malicious glance in Alice's direction, which didn't even ruffle her feathers. She knew now that Mark didn't have any romantic interest in his helpful neighbor, but it did bother Alice that Ethel was apparently suspicious of her feelings for Mark. They had to be sure that everything in their relationship was circumspect, for she was praying for Mark's return to the ministry; therefore, no hint of scandal should taint his reputation.

Before they left, Alice invited Gran to help her supervise sorting out the children's clothing. She'd observed that their closets were packed with clothing on hangers and stored in boxes, and much of it should be discarded, but she hesitated to do it by herself. She'd gotten Mark's permission to clear out items that the children no longer could wear and figure out what they'd need before school started.

Gran was obviously pleased to be included in the project, which took most of the day. They tackled Kristin's closet and dresser drawers first, and that took the whole morning, for Kristin was reluctant to part with some garments that were much too small for her to wear anymore. Eddie was more pliable— as long as they didn't bother his car collection, he didn't care what they threw away.

It was late afternoon by the time the discarded clothing was stuffed into garbage bags, and Alice put the bags into her van to take to the used clothing center operated by a downtown church. As she and the children drove into town on Chippenham Parkway, Kristin pointed to a three-story brick structure and said, "That's the bank where Daddy works."

Alice hadn't known the location of the bank, but when she noticed how close it was to the distribution center where they were going, she said, "I'm too tired to cook dinner tonight. Let's telephone your father and see if he'll take us out to eat."

"Hamburgers and French fries?" Eddie said.

"I suppose that would be all right, since all we had for lunch was fruit and yogurt. But your father might need more food than that."

"Then he can have two hamburgers," Eddie said, giggling.

"I'll telephone from the distribution center and see if he can join us."

After they carried the bags into the church basement and received a receipt for the items, should Mark want to deduct the amount from his income tax, Alice asked permission to use the telephone. She carried his phone number in her purse in case of emergencies, although she hadn't had reason to call him before. She waited breathlessly for him to answer, feeling downright giddy and flustered.

"Hi, Mark," she said when he answered. "This is Alice, and nothing is wrong," she hastened to assure him.

"This is an unexpected pleasure—the first time I've heard your voice on the phone."

Oh, please, Mark!

"We've spent the day cleaning closets, and we brought the discarded items to the church close to your office. We've been so busy I haven't had time to prepare any dinner, and we're wondering if we can find someone to take three hungry people out for dinner."

She could envision a smile spreading across his face, for since they'd acknowledged their growing feelings, he smiled often.

"I volunteer. Where do you want to go?"

"I heard hamburgers and French fries mentioned."

"Oh, we can do better than that. I'll take you to a nice restaurant."

"That wouldn't be a good idea. All three of us look scruffy. We'd better take a rain check on the nice restaurant."

"We'll compromise. I know a place that serves hamburgers and French fries, but also dinners. And there's an adjacent playground that the kids will like. I'll meet you at the church parking lot in a half hour." Alice was pleased that she'd thought of this—she mustn't damage Mark's self-esteem by always giving and not taking. And the evening meal shouldn't be too expensive.

"Okay. I'll telephone Gran to tell her our plans and that we'll bring her dinner."

To pass the time while they waited for Mark, Alice encouraged the two children to walk with her around the quiet neighborhood where the church was located. Mark was punctual, arriving soon after they returned from their walk. Kristin rushed to sit with Mark in the front seat, and with an apologetic shrug, Mark met Alice's eyes. With a nod she indicated that she understood.

"Why does Kristin always get to ride in the front seat?"

"Wait until you're a little larger, Son, and then you can take your turn." He stepped out of the car and removed his tie and coat.

"I might as well be comfortable like the rest of you," he said, observing their shorts and sleeveless shirts with envy.

A ten-minute drive on Midlothian Turnpike brought them to a restaurant that pleased all of them. The children's favorite foods were available; Mark ordered a shrimp dinner, and Alice chose roast beef.

It seemed strange that Eddie sat with Alice, while Kristin wanted to be beside her father. Eddie talked more than he had at first, but he was still quieter than Kristin, who chatted to her father about their day's experience. As they waited for their food, Alice observed her adopted family. All three of them had gained weight since she'd come to them, and certainly the improvement in Eddie was almost miraculous. Since Alice had kept him outside much of the time, his pasty white complexion had given way to a slight tan, tinged by rosy cheeks.

"Did you give all of your clothes away or do you still have some left?" Mark asked with a grin after listening to Kristin's account of the big sacks they'd brought to the church.

"I'll need some school clothes," Kristin said.

"She's outgrown most of her things," Alice said, "but Eddie can still wear a lot of his. We'll need to go shopping, but not for another couple of months." She tried to forestall any worries he might have about financing their school clothes. Alice had never seen him so relaxed, and she wanted him to stay that way.

As she ate the succulent roast beef, Alice said,

"This does taste good. I must be tired of my own cooking."

"You'll have to forgive me, Alice," Mark apologized. "I've not been thinking straight lately. We'll start eating out at least once a week."

"I wasn't complaining, but this is a nice experience."

The children asked permission to go out and play on the swings before Alice and Mark finished their meal, and Mark excused them.

"What kind of work do you do at the bank?"

"I'm in charge of personnel. It was fortunate for me that when I needed employment, the head of the Personnel Department retired."

"Do you like the work?"

"Yes, I do. I enjoy working with people, and I have the opportunity to do some counseling, which I've been trained to do. I supervise the employees in the main bank, as well as their branch facilities. I have more than a hundred employees to deal with—it's time-consuming, but when I'm at work, I don't fret about my other problems."

"I know it isn't any of my business, but when do you intend to return to the ministry?"

He covered her hand with his, and his feelings for her were evident by the intensity of his expression. "Anything you want to know about me *is* your business, but I don't know the answer." He squeezed her fingers and she returned the clasp. "It's a question that's in my mind all the time. I took a vow to serve the Lord with my whole life, and although I feel that the work I'm doing is worthwhile, it's not what God called me to do. I've lost enthusiasm for His work,

Alice, and until that returns, I can't go back to the pulpit.''

Their conversation was interrupted when Kristin came back to their table, with Eddie walking behind, his head down, and Alice quickly disengaged their hands. Eddie slid into the seat and snuggled over to Alice—she put her arm around him and held him close.

"Eddie's afraid," Kristin said in a haughty voice. "He won't get on the swings and the slide. He's no fun to play with."

"You wouldn't remember, Kristin, but the first time you went to a playground, you were afraid, too. We're finished now, and we'll come out and play with you."

When they got outside, Mark said, "Let's try the swings first, Son. You get on the seat, and I'll push the swing, but not too high."

Kristin jumped in one of the swings and propelled herself up and down. Her achievements intimidated Eddie.

"Let Alice hold me," he begged.

"I'm too heavy to sit in a swing. Just hold on to the chain, and you won't fall."

Eddie shook his head, and Mark said, "These are heavy-duty swings, and you shouldn't overload them, Alice, if you want to swing with him."

"I'm heavier than you think," Alice said with a laugh. "We may have to pay for a damaged swing, but I'll try it. Come on, Eddie."

She sat down and lifted Eddie to her lap. Slowly, Mark pushed the swing, and Alice helped their progress with her feet. She sensed Eddie relaxing.

"I like it. Go higher, Daddy."

Alice looked over her shoulder and Mark grinned at her. "You're right—you are heavier than you look." She made a face at him.

After about ten minutes, Eddie agreed he could manage without Alice's help, so she went to watch Kristin enjoy herself on the slide. When Mark and Eddie joined them, Eddie whined, "I can't do that—I'm afraid."

"You don't have to play on the slide," Mark said, "if you don't want to."

"I want to play, but I'm afraid."

Mark checked out the small slide. "There are only six steps to the top, Eddie. If Alice stands behind you, and I catch you when you come down the slide—do you think you can do it?"

"I don't know."

"Let's try," Alice said, "I'll climb up the steps behind you, but I'm not trying the slide," she stated in response to Mark's amused expression and his uplifted eyebrows.

Eddie trembled by the time he climbed the six rungs on the ladder, and even when he got situated at the top, he wouldn't budge from his perch. Alice climbed until she could peer over the slide at Mark.

"I'll give him a little push. Be ready to catch him." She gently unlocked Eddie's hands from the sides of the slide and gave him a nudge, holding on to him as long as she could. He screamed, and though he made it into Mark's arms safely, Eddie's face was white and his lips trembled.

"I don't want to slide anymore, Daddy. I'd rather swing."

Alice sat on a nearby bench while Mark took Eddie to the swings, and Kristin played alone on the slide. When Eddie learned how to swing alone, Mark joined her on the bench, their shoulders touching lightly.

An elderly couple came out of the restaurant and stood watching the two children for a few minutes. The woman turned and spoke to Mark. "You have a lovely family. We've been watching you while you played with them. You must be proud of your children."

Alice gasped slightly and lowered her head, but Mark replied steadily, "Why, yes, we are proud of them, thank you. They're fine children."

Alice got up and wandered to where Eddie was swinging, and after the couple moved on, Mark joined her.

"What else could I say? We are proud of them, aren't we?" he said with a shrug. "I didn't think explanations were necessary."

Knowing that the farm activities might not be enough entertainment for Kristin and Eddie, Alice packed the softball and bat, and a badminton set she'd found among the cartons in her bedroom. She took her portable television along in case the children wanted to watch a program in their rooms. She knew they wouldn't lack for food at the farm, but she bought some pudding cups, potato chips and a few two-liter bottles of cola as special treats.

Mark helped her pack the van the night before they left.

"I'm going to miss you—all of you," he added meaningfully.

"I do feel guilty taking your kids away from you

for a week. I was thinking of the good it would do them, not considering how it would affect you.''

''Oh, I wasn't feeling sorry for myself. I want them to have this experience, but I'll be lonely.''

Without looking directly at him, Alice said, ''Look on the bright side—Ethel will be here to keep you company.''

He grinned at her, his dimple deepening—it was obvious that she had nothing to fear from Ethel.

''You'll come to the farm for the weekend, won't you?''

''If I don't get involved in something at the bank that keeps me late, I'll come Friday evening. I'll call and let you know.''

Chapter Five

As they traveled, Eddie importantly taught his sister the game he and Alice had played when they'd gone to the church camp. That kept them occupied for a while, and when they started fussing, Alice produced some puzzle books and pencils. To break the ride, she stopped at a roadside park that had a few playthings for children, and to eat the picnic lunch that she had packed. They arrived at the farm in midafternoon.

The hundred-acre farm was in the Piedmont region of Virginia. The buildings were located along a lazy river meandering through the middle of the farm, fed from the wooded hills to the north. About half of the farm was arable, and it was planted in corn and soya beans. In addition to the two-story dwelling, there was a large barn, garage, and a chicken house. As they drove along the lane that took them to the farmstead, Alice observed with pleasure the neat fields, and the new-mown pasture fields behind the barn. Her uncle was a good farmer.

Landon Wilcox wasn't a handsome man, for above his freckled face was a thatch of wild and unruly red hair. His long drooping nose was high at the bridge giving his face a beaklike appearance, but his gray eyes sparkled mischievously, indicative of his jovial personality. He sat on the wide veranda that surrounded the old house. When he came off the porch to greet them, a basset hound and a half-dozen puppies ran after him. By the time petite, fair-haired Margaret came out of the house, Kristin and Eddie had dropped to the ground, and the pups were climbing all over them.

Laughing, Alice said, "I see you've added some new livestock to the farm. And I was afraid there wouldn't be enough to keep the kids from being bored!"

Landon gave her a bear hug, and Alice stooped to kiss Aunt Margaret. "So these are the children you're caring for?" Margaret said.

"Eddie, Kristin, leave the dogs alone for a few minutes and meet my relatives."

Eddie and Kristin both held a puppy in their arms, but they stood up, the other pups yipping and chewing on their shoes and socks.

"This is my Aunt Margaret and Uncle Landon. We're going to be their guests for the week."

Eddie stuck out his little hand toward Landon. "I'm Eddie Tanner."

Smothering a smile, Landon shook his hand. "Glad to meet you, Eddie. We don't have any boys around here, so you'll have to help me on the farm this week."

"What are we supposed to call you?" Kristin asked.

"Whatever you want to, dear," Margaret said.

"Then we'll call you Aunt Margaret and Uncle Landon, just like Alice does. We don't have any uncles at all, and only one aunt, and she lives in Tennessee so we don't see her very often."

Eddie again dropped to the ground to play with the puppies, and he looked up at Landon, his eyes bright and hopeful.

"Can we have one of the puppies, please?"

Landon glanced at Alice.

"That's a decision for your daddy to make, but don't get your hopes up. He may not want to adopt a puppy." She looked at Margaret. "Mark, the children's father and my employer, may come up over the weekend. I hope that'll be all right."

Margaret nodded, and Landon said, "The more the merrier. Come on, Eddie, let's take a ride on the tractor. I have to plow a section of the garden this afternoon."

"Can I take the puppy?"

"Not on the tractor. You can play with the puppy after supper."

"Don't I get to ride on the tractor?" Kristin asked.

"Sure thing," Landon said, "but only one kid at a time."

Reluctantly, Eddie and Kristin released their puppies, and the mother dog waddled back to the porch, her brood awkwardly following her.

"Let me put some sunscreen on you, Eddie—I don't want you to get a sunburn." Alice rummaged in the back of the van to find the bag she'd packed for emergencies, and after she rubbed his arms and legs generously with the lotion, she said, "I wish I'd brought a cap for him."

"He can wear one of my straw hats," Landon said.

"Kristin," Margaret said, "you come and help me string green beans for supper, and you can ride on the tractor tomorrow."

As Alice unpacked the van, she saw Eddie following Landon out to the garden. The sight of the boy with the big straw hat flopping down over his ears was hilarious, and she grabbed her camera. She'd noticed very few pictures at the Tanners, and she intended to record their activities this summer. She snapped a picture from the rear, and when he turned, she got a close-up of his face, barely visible under the floppy brim.

Eddie was skittish of climbing on the tractor, but Landon had grandchildren, and he knew how to calm the boy's fears. Alice was sure he'd waited until their arrival to plow the garden to give Eddie a chance to ride the tractor.

Landon placed Eddie on the seat before him, and Alice paused to watch. Eddie put his little hands beside the hairy freckled hands of Landon, and when he saw Alice looking their way, he straightened his back and yelled over the tractor's roaring motor, "Look at me, Alice. I'm driving. Take my picture." Alice was glad she'd bought several extra rolls of film.

She carried all their luggage upstairs and placed it in the three rooms Margaret had prepared. Afterward, she located Kristin and Margaret on the back porch, where Kristin was slowly getting the knack of snapping the long green beans. She took a picture of that activity, too—partly to have mementos for the children, but also so Mark wouldn't miss altogether what his children were doing.

When bedtime came, Alice realized that she'd forgotten to pack one very important item—a nightlight. When they started upstairs, Kristin peered out the living room window.

"It's dark outside. I can't see anything. And you can't hear any sounds at all."

Eddie didn't comment, but he edged close to Alice, and clutched her jeans as they walked upstairs.

She showed the children to their bedrooms, where she'd laid out their pj's on the bed. Kristin and Eddie tiptoed around, only adding to the quietness. The rooms, with their high ceilings and antique wooden furniture intimidated the children. When Eddie climbed into the full-size bed, he did look awfully small.

"We'll leave the bathroom light on tonight," Alice told him as she bent and kissed his cheek. "And I'm in the room across the hall—there's nothing to be afraid of."

He nodded solemnly, but his blue eyes looked enormous in the dim light.

Alice paused at Kristin's open door. "Are you all right?"

"I think so. What are those funny sounds outdoors?"

"Night insects—katydids and locusts, and lots of other kinds I can't recognize. They're in cities, too, but we can't hear them because of the traffic and other noises."

Alice turned off the hall light, but left the bathroom light on to keep the children from being afraid. She undressed in the darkness, and slipped between the sheets. The farmhouse wasn't air-conditioned, and she welcomed the breeze drifting through the open window.

Alice lay with her hands behind her head, propped up on the pillow, not the least bit sleepy. She hadn't been here to stay overnight since her marriage ten years ago. What a lot had happened to her in that length of time. Married and widowed. The last time she slept in this bed, she'd never heard of Mark Tanner, and in spite of the thirty-five years she'd lived before she met Mark, it seemed as if her life had only started two months ago when she'd entered his home.

"Alice." Her thoughts were interrupted by Eddie's timorous voice. He stood in the doorway. She sat up in bed.

"Yes. What is it?"

"I'm scared. It's awful quiet, but still I can hear squeaking sounds. I can't go to sleep. Maybe we ought to go home."

"But if we go home, you wouldn't be here to ride the pony tomorrow. You don't want to miss that."

He didn't answer, but Alice thought she heard a sniff.

With a quiet sigh, she said, "Would you like to crawl in beside me for a while?"

His bare feet pattered across the floor, and she reached out a hand to lift him into the bed. With a little giggle, he scooted across the mattress, until he was pressed close against her side.

"You smell good, Alice, and you're soft and cuddly just like my bear."

"That's quite a compliment."

"Can I come, too?" Kristin's voice sounded from the hallway.

"Don't tell me you're afraid?"

"No, but that's an awful big bed for just me."

Alice turned back the bed covers. "Come on."

The two children were soon asleep, but Alice lay between them unable to settle down. Betty would have a fit if she knew Alice permitted her charges to sleep with her—no doubt it was against nanny rules. But her growing love for Mark extended to his children, and she found it difficult to refuse their requests. *Where was this going to end?* Mark had made it plain that remarriage wasn't in his plans. What did the future hold for her? Was she drifting into deep water from which there wasn't any return?

On their second evening at the farm, Mark telephoned while they were eating supper, and Alice's hand itched to take the phone when Landon said who was calling. She stayed in her chair while Kristin and Eddie ran to get the receiver—Kristin winning as usual. Eddie hopped from one foot to the other as his sister talked, and grabbed the phone with alacrity when it was his turn.

Mark must have asked if he was having a good time, for he said, "Yes, I am, Daddy. I've been driving the tractor, riding the pony, and playing with the puppies. And we're waiting until you come Saturday to go on a picnic in the woods. Uncle Landon calls it a hayride."

Alice could envision Mark's eyes lighting as he listened to Eddie's ramblings.

"Alice, Daddy wants to talk to you."

Careful, she thought as she left the table. Aunt

Margaret is pretty shrewd—she'll catch on quickly.
But she couldn't keep a lilt out of her voice when
she answered.

"How are things going? The kids sound as if
they're having a good time."

"All of us are."

"Then they haven't worn you out completely?"

"Not at all. We're sorry that you can't be with us,
too. How's Gran getting along?"

"Fine. She had most of dinner ready when I got
home tonight. Ethel was all set to come every day,
but I rather forcefully dispensed with her services. I
told her if she wanted to be of help, she could check
on Gran over the weekend."

"I'm sure that wasn't the kind of service she had
in mind."

"She's pretty hard to discourage, but I want you
to know I've tried."

"I believe it."

Alice gave him directions on how to find the farm
and handed the phone back to Kristin, who had stood
nearby listening intently.

The rest of the week passed quickly, and the children retained their enthusiasm for rural life. Alice
and Landon took them fishing; Margaret kept them
fed well with fresh-baked cookies and other pastries,
and both children enjoyed riding the lazy pony
around the barn lot. It was only at night that they
seemed to miss their father, and when they were
ready for bed, as a matter of course, they went into
Alice's room and got in her bed.

She wanted them to enjoy their week, and since
she wasn't heartless enough to force them to sleep
in their rooms, she turned the time to good use. After

they got in bed, and before she turned off the light, she put her arms around both of them and told them Bible stories. Their favorite was the time Jesus had called the little children to him and blessed them, and they wanted to hear that every night.

"When we visited the Holy Land several years ago, we saw the places that Jesus visited and where He might have been when He blessed the children. He probably sat on a little hill overlooking the Sea of Galilee."

"Is that a pretty place?" Kristin asked.

"The hillsides aren't as pretty and green as we have here in Virginia, but any place Jesus has been is beautiful."

"Have you been lots of places?"

"Yes, I have, Kristin. My husband was associated with the state department, and before his illness, he had many occasions to travel in foreign countries. I always went with him, and after he finished his work, he took a week or so of vacation, and we went sight-seeing."

"What happened to your husband?" Eddie asked.

"He died and went to be with the Lord."

"Just like our Mommy," Eddie said. "Are you sad, too, Alice?"

"I used to be, but not since I've had the two of you to take care of."

"And Daddy, too?"

Alice's heart beat like a jackhammer at the question, but she managed to answer lightly. "Daddy doesn't actually need taking care of. He's big enough to look out for himself."

Once the story time was finished, Kristin and Eddie slept soundly, but Alice didn't. For one thing,

Eddie was restless and turned frequently, usually
yanking the bedcovers with him. Also, she was troubled. If she was a good nanny, she would know how
to reassure these children and put them in their separate beds. But a good nanny wouldn't have fallen
in love with her charges' father, either. Why had she
listened to Betty? Why hadn't she returned to teaching? That way she could have worked with children
during the day, and they would have returned to their
parents at night, and her heart wouldn't have been
involved.

Alice was also worried about the weekend. She
was so eager to see Mark that she could hardly bear
to wait the hours away before he arrived. Could she
possibly conceal her feelings for Mark from Margaret
and Landon? If her pulse raced when she even
thought about Mark, how would her emotions stir
when she saw him after a few days' separation?

Lying in the bed she'd slept in when she was a
child, she remembered the times she'd prayed for
guidance in her life. As soon as she recognized the
Lordship of Christ, Alice knew He had a purpose for
her, and she thought that meant becoming a mother.
Had she mistaken His leadership when she married
John Larkin? She'd never doubted that she would
have children, but it was a subject they hadn't discussed before marriage, and she didn't know until
later that John was reluctant to take on the responsibility of a young family at his age. Alice hadn't
insisted.

Mark planned to arrive by six o'clock on Friday,
and two hours before his arrival, Kristin and Eddie
sat on the front steps watching the road for his ve-

hicle. They played with the puppies crawling all over them, pulling at their clothes, but they kept alert for the sound of Mark's station wagon. Alice had decided not to be present when he arrived, and she was in the dining room setting the table when he came.

Each of them carrying a pup, the kids bounded off the porch when Mark's vehicle rounded the bend. Alice pulled back the curtain in the dining room to watch their reunion.

Mark stooped and put his arms around them, seeming to savor their kisses and the drooling tongues of the two pups. His eyes scanned the front of the house and, with a quickening heartbeat, Alice knew he was looking for her.

Landon came up behind her, having just finished shaving, and she said, "Come out and meet Mark Tanner, Uncle. You'll like him."

"He's raised two nice kids, I'll say that for him."

In Landon's company, Alice knew she would be less self-conscious, and her voice didn't betray her inner turmoil when they met Mark at the bottom of the steps.

"Uncle Landon, this is Mark Tanner. Landon Wilcox, my uncle."

The men shook hands, but before they could say much, Kristin said, "We want to take a puppy home with us, Daddy. Uncle Landon said we could have one—they're old enough to leave their mother now."

"But Alice said you'd have to decide," Eddie said.

Mark looked at her then, and his blue eyes gleamed. "Well, thanks a lot." To the children, he said, "I'll think about it, and then we'll have a talk. There's a lot of work involved in adopting a puppy."

Margaret came out on the porch to greet Mark, and when the children wanted to take him to see the pony, she said, "Not until we've eaten supper. Eddie, show your daddy upstairs to the bathroom, so he can refresh himself after his journey."

When they entered the house, and Mark saw the steep flight of steps, he looked at Alice questioningly. She nodded significantly. Eddie grabbed Mark's hand and pulled him toward the stairs. Mark looked over his shoulder at Alice and shook his head in wonder.

In a low voice, Alice explained to Landon and Margaret, "Two months ago, Eddie couldn't have climbed the steps without help, and even then, he would have gasped for breath."

"He's stronger than when he came here," Landon said.

"That's the reason I imposed our company on you this week. I thought a vacation on the farm would be good for both of them."

"You're always welcome, you know that," Margaret said.

Alice helped Margaret clear the table and wash the dishes while the kids took Mark to see the pony and to demonstrate their expertise in riding. Later, all of them sat on the front porch and visited. Alice sat in the swing and gently swayed back and forth, saying very little, content to let Mark and Landon do the talking. She was pleased with how well they got on together, and jubilant that Mark was relaxed, and seemingly as carefree as the children.

Hoping for a few minutes to talk with Mark about the sleeping arrangements, and while the children were playing badminton, she said, "Before it's completely dark, Mark, you should bring in your luggage. I'll show you your room."

"I have only one suitcase." He walked down to the car with a jaunty step.

Walking side by side up the wide stairs, she said quietly, "I've had a bit of problem with the children at night. When night falls, it's *dark* here, and I didn't bring a night-light. The first night, they were afraid and wanted to sleep with me, and I allowed it, which was a mistake—they've accepted that as the status quo."

"They shouldn't impose on you that way."

"It was strange for them here, and they missed you, so I didn't have the heart to make them sleep alone."

"You have to be firm with them."

"I'm glad to hear you say that. You can explain that to them tonight, and I'm sure they'll hop right in their beds and go to sleep immediately. I'm a softie, and I can't be firm like you."

He grinned at her, and his dimple deepened. "Don't be sarcastic. At least, I'll take Eddie off your hands tonight. Where do you want us to sleep?"

She turned into the bedroom Eddie had vacated on the first night. "Whew!" he said. "This *is* a big room—no wonder he was afraid."

Alice raised the window. "The house isn't air-conditioned, and with the window open, the kids heard lots of strange insect sounds—that bothered them."

"We'll be comfortable tonight."

"I wouldn't count on it—Eddie kicks like a mule. If you need to hang up your clothes, there are hangers in the closet. Come on down when you're ready."

Mark took her by the arm. She shook her head and moved toward the door. A look of frustration crossed his face, and he jammed his hands in his pockets.

"Words can't express how I feel about you, Alice. If I didn't care for you for yourself, I'd fall in love with you for the change you've brought about in my kids. When I consider how they were when you came to us and look at them now, it's overwhelming."

"Everything I do for them, I'm doing for you, Mark."

She left the room hurriedly before he could say anything more. They'd both said too much already.

"'Old McDonald had a farm, ee-ii-ee-ii-oo, And on this farm he had some ducks, ee-ii-ee-ii-oo. With a quack-quack here, and a quack-quack there…'"

Jolting along the farm road in a wagon pulled by Landon's tractor wasn't conducive to good singing, but the five passengers belted out the words of the old song anyway. Landon had put a few bales of hay in the small wagon, and Margaret, Alice, Mark and the children were wedged in around the bales and two large picnic baskets, surrounded by the smell of recently fried chicken.

The wagon entered the woods, and climbed steadily along the side of the hill until they reached a wide, level clearing. Large oaks and maples overhung the roadway, making a canopy for their travel.

"I'll spread our blankets under the trees," Margaret said, "and we'll eat in about an hour."

"Let's play for a while," Alice said. "I brought the ball and bat."

"What if I get hit in the belly again?" Eddie said, his face whitening.

Mark tousled his hair. "When you see a ball heading for your tummy, step out of the way."

"Are you going to play, Uncle Landon?" Kristin said.

"Might as well. Margaret won't give me anything to eat until the game's over."

After an hour of playing, they were ready for the fried chicken, vegetable sticks, baked beans and lemonade. Chocolate cake completed their picnic.

"Mrs. Wilcox," Mark said. "Alice must have learned to cook from you. She's a great cook, but I believe your fried chicken is even better than hers—maybe you'd better give her some more lessons."

Alice threw a carrot stick at him, which he caught and put in his mouth. "For that remark, I may let you do your own cooking again."

"No, Alice," Eddie said firmly. "Your food tastes better than Daddy's."

"Well, I know when I'm beaten," Mark said. "I'll just have to settle for mediocre chicken." He stretched. "Hey, kids, let's take a walk through the woods."

"You coming, too, Alice?" Eddie asked.

"Not this time. I'll keep Aunt Margaret company, for Uncle Landon will be asleep in a short time."

When the Tanners were out of hearing, Margaret said, "What happened to Mark's wife?"

Alice leaned against the huge maple that shaded them. "She died about eight months ago, but she'd had cancer for two years before that. Mark has had a rough time, trying to take care of her and the children, especially since Eddie has been sick, too."

"I believe the boy's come out of it," Landon said.

"The doctor says his heart is all right now, but he's still behind physically and emotionally. We're trying to build him up so he can go to kindergarten this fall."

"How long do you intend to stay at the Tanners'?" Margaret said.

"I don't know. I went on a month's trial, and now that I'm committed, I intend to stay as long as they need me."

"You're sacrificing your own life for another's family. I don't know why you're doing it."

Alice had expected Aunt Margaret to understand her reasons, but apparently she didn't.

"I haven't had such a great life the past few years. During John's sickness, I was confined to the house, and for a year, I've been at a standstill. It's a pleasure to see the Tanner children's improvement, and Gran's, too, for that matter."

"How is Gran related to the Tanners?" Margaret asked.

"She's the children's great-grandmother, and they're the closest living relatives she has. I wanted her to come with us, but she's badly handicapped from a stroke, and she decided it was best for her to stay at home."

"Don't get too involved with the Tanners," Margaret advised. "It could lead to heartache."

"Tend to your own business, Margaret," Landon said. "Can't you see that Alice is happier than she's been for years? Let her make her own decisions."

Alice threw her uncle a grateful glance, which he didn't see because he was flat on his back, his straw hat covering his face.

"By the way, as far as Mark knows, I have to work for a living. Please don't tell him otherwise."

After supper, Landon and Margaret went to the living room to watch their favorite Saturday night television programs. Mark and Alice played badminton with the children until it was almost dark, then Alice got two small jars from the cellar and showed the children how to catch lightning bugs, and put them in the jars to make their own lights. When they tired of this, Alice took the lids off the jars, so the bugs could escape. She sat down in the swing, and Eddie snuggled down beside her, laid his head in her lap, and the gentle swaying of the swing soon put him to sleep.

Yawning, Kristin stretched out on the porch floor beside the sleeping basset hound and pups. Mark sat in a rocking chair close to Alice, and he drew a deep breath.

"It's peaceful here. When I first entered the ministry, I hoped to serve in a country parish."

Lord, give me the right words. "It isn't too late, Mark. It isn't difficult to find a rural pastorate, for the majority of ministers prefer to serve in cities and towns."

Without commenting, Mark rocked slowly back and forth. "Both of the kids are asleep. Suppose we should put them to bed?"

"It's early yet. It's been hot today, so let's wait a little longer for the upstairs to cool."

"Alice, I'd like to hear about your marriage," Mark said quietly. "Do you mind?"

Galloping horses and the squeaking wheels of a stagecoach from the house indicated that the Wilcoxes were still engrossed in their Western show. Alice halted the swing, groping for words.

"John Larkin was thirty years older than I, and he was the father of my best college friend. I went home with Martha numerous weekends and was accepted as one of the family. Her mother had been dead several years. Right before we graduated from college, Martha was killed in an automobile accident. She was his only child, and her death devastated John."

Alice swung back and forth for a while, and her hand on Eddie's side monitored the soft rise and fall of his breathing, as she relived that tragedy. She'd been heartbroken when Martha was killed.

"He insisted on keeping in close contact with me, and I continued to visit him. John seemed to transfer his paternal devotion to me, and I thought that was all there was to our relationship until he asked me to marry him."

"Perhaps I shouldn't have asked. I'll understand if you don't want to discuss it. I'm not being nosy—it's important for me to know."

She held out her hand and he caressed it tenderly while she talked.

"I was shocked at first, for I'd never thought of him romantically. I'd considered all of his attention to me as a catharsis for Martha's loss. It scared me, and I backed off—didn't see him for several months. At that time, I didn't know how important love was to a marriage, and I finally agreed to marry John. My parents had a fit—you see, John was older than they were—but they became reconciled to it. If I had the decision to make over again, I don't know what I'd do."

"You didn't love him?"

"Not the way you mean. I respected him, and we did have a good marriage. He was very kind and considerate—I wasn't unhappy, but..."

"But?"

"It wasn't long before I knew that I wanted more from marriage, but it was too late to change. When John became ill, I had plenty to occupy my mind, and I didn't think about what might have been."

"You're a kind and compassionate person, Alice, giving up your youth to help the father of your friend recover from her death, and you sacrificed again to nurse and care for him. In the same way, you've given up your own comfort for my family—I don't know how much you've sacrificed for us, but I'm beginning to think it's quite a lot. I've never known anyone like you, Alice."

He'd moved his chair closer to the swing while she talked, and he lifted the hand he held to his lips.

Alice stirred under his gesture, but she withdrew her hand. The only way she could possibly continue her position as a nanny was to rebuff, or at least, discourage Mark's overtures. But to do so was the hardest thing Alice had ever dealt with, for she yearned to give him everything he needed—not only financially but emotionally. She couldn't get Erin's appraisal of Clarice out of her mind, but even if she'd been an affectionate woman before her illness, Alice surmised that it had been more than two years since Mark had experienced any tenderness from anyone— always giving out, and getting nothing in return. It was little wonder he'd despaired to the point of almost forsaking God.

"We should be getting the children in bed," Alice said.

"I hope I haven't offended you," Mark said.

"You know better than that," Alice whispered. "I can't give way to my real feelings. I'm still trying to put the welfare of others before what I want. Kristin and Eddie aren't ready to share you yet."

He nodded and released her hand. She nudged Eddie awake. "Time to get in bed, Eddie. We have to get up a little earlier to get ready for church. Remember, we're going to the church I attended when I was a little girl."

Eddie stirred, sat up, and dangled his feet over the edge of the swing. "Is Daddy going with us?"

"I don't know—you'll have to ask him."

Mark helped Eddie dress for church, and Alice wondered if he might go with them, for instead of shorts and knit shirt like he'd worn yesterday, he came to breakfast in dress slacks and a blue sport shirt, but she didn't ask. Since the Wilcoxes' only vehicle was a pickup truck, they were all going in the van. Mark stood on the porch and watched as the others climbed into the vehicle. Although she'd decided Mark couldn't be pressured in the important spiritual decisions he must make, before she got into the driver's seat, she walked back to the porch where he leaned against one of the pillars.

"I could use a chauffeur." She held out her keys.

He wouldn't meet her eyes, and she thought he would refuse. When he finally reached out and took the keys, she wanted to throw her arms around him, but conscious of the four sets of watching eyes behind them, Alice turned and took the rear seat in the van beside Kristin.

"I'm glad Daddy's going with us," the girl whispered.

"So am I."

The church was located two miles away, in a shady grove along the same river that flowed through the farm. "We used to have picnics once a month during the summer, and the kids looked forward to them," Alice said.

Although Alice was pleased to have Mark attend church with them, she couldn't help fear that someone might drop a remark that would reveal her financial status.

So, instead of saying that she was the children's nanny, she introduced the Tanners as "Mark Tanner and his children—friends of mine." Even that introduction caused a few raised eyebrows, but at least no one would be saying, "A nanny—what happened to your money? I didn't suppose you'd ever have to work again."

To forestall any speculation among her former neighbors, Alice arranged to have Mark sit beside Landon, with the two children beside him, and for Margaret to sit between her and Kristin and Eddie.

Before they'd left the farm, she'd told Kristin and Eddie that they wouldn't have a separate service, but would have to sit in the sanctuary with the adults. But the minister did have a story time for the children, and with Mark's encouragement, his two children went forward with the others.

Alice's hands clenched during the hymn preceding the sermon, and her heart wept for Mark's anguish, when the congregation sang, "I've Wandered Far Away From God, But Now I'm Coming Home." And when the minister read the text for his sermon,

"'Father, I have sinned against heaven and against you. I am no more worthy to be called your son,'" she knew Mark was in for a rough morning. But she believed this service was part of God's plan to bring Mark back to his ordained place in the ministry. Perhaps the gentle wooing of the Spirit would come more easily to Mark from this stranger than from one of his former colleagues.

When the services ended, Landon directed Mark to drive back to the farm on a circuitous route that led past a waterfall and an abandoned gristmill. The chatter of Margaret and the children as they passed these sites covered Mark's silence, but Alice, sensitive to all of his moods, was convinced that the morning's message was speaking to his heart.

Chapter Six

When they drove into the farmyard, a compact car stood behind Mark's station wagon. Alice recognized it at once, and glancing at the porch, she saw her parents coming down the steps to meet them. Alice looked quickly at Margaret.

"Did you know they were coming today?"

Margaret smiled wryly. "No, but they did know you would be here this week, so I'm not too surprised."

She meant to convey a message to Mark when she said, "Well, kids, you're going to meet my mother and father."

"It's fun to meet so many new people," Kristin said.

Alice wasn't pleased with her parents' presence, for they hadn't wanted her to take the nanny position, and she was sure they'd come to see what she'd gotten herself into. And short of coming to the Tanner house, how else could they have found out?

"Hi, Margaret," Harley Taylor called. "Got any extra fried chicken for two hungry people?"

"Not chicken, but we've got plenty of meat loaf," Margaret replied. "You're welcome."

Attempting to hide her annoyance, Alice greeted her parents, wishing as she often had since they'd moved away from the farm that they'd stayed more active. Retirement hadn't been good for either of them—they'd become sedentary and were gaining too much weight.

She turned to Mark, and the two children who watched curiously. "Mom, Dad, I want you to meet the Tanner family. This is Mark, Kristin and Eddie," she said, laying an affectionate hand on Eddie's curly hair. Meeting Mark's glance, she added, "Norma and Harley Taylor."

With uncommon jollity, Harley shook hands with Mark and the children. "So, our Alice has become your nanny. Has she paddled you yet?"

"No, sir," Eddie said, his blue eyes sparkling. "Alice is good to us. She lets us play games on her computer, and she fixes us real good meals."

"She took me to camp, and she plays games with us when Daddy's late getting home from work," Kristin added.

Alice flushed at their praise.

"We're fortunate to have Alice—she's done wonders with the children," Mark added.

"I'm sure she has," Norma spoke for the first time.

"Come on in the house," Landon said.

"I'll see that the children change clothes and pack their suitcases if you need to help Margaret," Mark said to Alice.

"I'll leave right after lunch and take the children with me, so you can have the rest of the day with your family."

"Thanks," she answered, not sure she wanted to be left to face her parents' inquisition.

Mealtime went very well, thanks to Landon, who had the knack of putting everyone at ease. Mark had recovered from the reflective mood that had gripped him since the morning's sermon, and he knew how to meet people at their own level by discussing what was important to them. Even Norma Taylor, whom Alice suspected had made up her mind not to like Mark, seemed impressed with him. No wonder Mark was so successful in the ministry—he loved people and was sincerely interested in their lives and aspirations. Alice thought of the song they'd sung this morning: "I've Wandered Far Away From God, But Now I'm Coming Home." She longed for the day when Mark would sing those words and mean them.

The only unpleasant part of the meal was when Eddie overturned a glass of tea into Alice's lap. His lips puckered, and Alice put her arms around him.

"Never mind, Eddie. That could have happened to any of us."

"But, Alice, I've ruined your pretty dress."

"No, you haven't!" She kissed Eddie on the forehead. "Here, help me soak up what's on the table and floor with these napkins, and then I'll change into something dry."

"You're still just a baby, Eddie," Kristin said.

"That's enough, Kristin," Mark said sternly. "I'll help Eddie clean up, Alice—you go ahead and change."

* * *

As soon as the meal was finished, Mark went upstairs for their luggage and packed it into the station wagon. As they prepared to leave, Eddie and Kristin both held a puppy, looking wistfully at their father. The subject of adopting a puppy had come up several times during the weekend, but Mark had been noncommittal to his children's pleas.

"Can we have one of the puppies, please?" Kristin asked.

Eddie didn't say anything, but clutched the puppy tightly, looking at his father hopefully.

"Oh, I don't know, kids." He looked at Alice. "What do you think? It will make extra work for you. You decide."

"Coward," she accused him, laughing. "You can have *one* of the puppies," she said to the children, "but you can't take it today. We'll have to make some arrangements to house the puppy, as well as lay down a few ground rules about who's going to take care of him. It'll be better for the puppy to stay with its mother for a few more days anyway. We'll come back in a couple of weeks, after the four of us have talked it over. Is that okay?"

Eddie rushed over to Alice, and still holding the pup, he threw his arms around her legs, as he often did, with such force that it staggered her. There wasn't any doubt he was becoming stronger. The puppy squealed.

"Thanks, Alice. Kristin and me'll take care of it. It won't make any more work for you."

"Famous last words," Mark said wryly, "but I thank you, too. They should have a pet, but the time has never seemed right."

Without prompting, Kristin and Eddie thanked

Margaret and Landon for the good visit. Mark shook hands with the Wilcoxes and the Taylors, and Alice walked down to the station wagon with them.

"I'll be home before too late," she said to Mark, knowing that wherever Mark Tanner was would be home to her from now on.

The kids waved gaily as Mark turned the station wagon into the roadway and headed toward Richmond.

"Nice kids," Harley said as Alice returned to the porch.

Hoping to forestall what her mother might say, Alice said, "We'd better take care of the dishes, Aunt Margaret. That was surely a good meal."

Margaret knew her sister as well as Alice did, and perhaps that was the reason she kept the conversation on impersonal subjects. After the dishes were washed and dried, Alice went upstairs to assemble her luggage—she intended to leave in time to be back in Richmond before nightfall. When she came downstairs, she joined the rest of them on the front porch.

"Nancy told me to tell you that she wants to take her kids to the beach house for a couple of weeks. She thought you could come, too, and Harley and I might be there some of the time."

"She's welcome to go, of course, but ask her to let me know when she's going. Although I haven't cleared it with Mark, I intend to take the children and Gran to the beach for a week before school starts, but I won't come the same time you're there. Kristin and Eddie are so much younger than Nancy's children that they wouldn't be compatible."

"And is Mark going to the beach, too?" her mother queried.

"I doubt he'll be able to get away. He's worked at the bank less than a year, so he doesn't have any vacation time."

"I certainly liked Mark," Landon said easily. "He's a fine man and a great father."

"But why did he leave the ministry—that's what I'd like to know?" Harley said. Everyone looked to Alice for an answer.

"I'm not going to discuss Mark's affairs with you—as a matter of fact, he hasn't told me why he left the ministry. I'm only a nanny to his children, and as such, I have no right to meddle in his past."

"Just how long do you intend to stay with the Tanners?" Norma asked.

"My contract says that either of us can rescind my employment with two weeks' notice. But I went there because Betty St. Claire convinced me I was needed, and I intend to stay as long as I can be of help."

"Be of help!" Norma said indignantly. "It sounds to me as if you're little more than a slave."

"I set my own workload, Mom, and I'm happier than I've been for a long time, so let's leave it that way. Okay?"

Norma didn't answer, but rolled her eyes significantly.

"Sister," Margaret said to Norma, "I think you're overreacting to the situation. Alice certainly knows what she wants to do. She isn't a child."

"No," Norma agreed, "it would be better if she were. Can't the rest of you see that she's in love with Mark Tanner, and that she's become a mother to those children?" Turning to Alice, she said, "If you're already so attached to them in two months, what's going to happen if you stay there any longer? Or are you intending to marry him? It isn't decent for you to live in the house with him. What must the neighbors think of the situation?''

''Believe me, we're well chaperoned with two children and Gran in the house at all times. In a city, it isn't unusual for a nanny to live in the home. Besides, I'm an employee—I get paid for the work I do.''

Landon laughed. ''This conversation sounds like something out of the Victorian era. Norma, your daughter is a widow, in her thirties, not a teenager that you need to advise. Are you sure your concern doesn't stem from the fact that you think Alice is spending more time with the Tanner children than with Jason and Polly?''

Norma's face reddened. ''Not necessarily, but I do think she should help Nancy and the children more.''

''I do help them!'' Alice protested. ''I've bought most of their clothing for years.''

''But you don't take them anywhere,'' Harley said.

''No, and I don't intend to until their behavior improves. They've always been willful children, and entering the teen years hasn't changed that.''

''You should have taken them on a cruise or to Europe this summer. It would have been a break for Nancy.''

''Let's change the subject,'' Landon said, and he asked questions about the retirement village where the Taylors lived. They were enthusiastic about their home, and Alice's situation was dropped for the moment.

Alice left the farm in early afternoon—sooner than

she had expected to, but she was reluctant to return to Richmond right away, so she drove northward and spent several hours visiting the Civil War battlefields of Chancellorsville and The Wilderness. Her mind was in such a turmoil after the scene with her parents that, when she got in the van and started toward Richmond, she didn't remember one thing she'd read on the many placards explaining the battles. It was past nine o'clock when she arrived at the Tanner home.

Mark came to the door to meet her.

"I was getting worried about you. Have a nice visit with your family?" he asked.

She laughed a little. "Not completely, but that isn't new. Mom doesn't always approve of what I do."

He walked down the hall with her. "I've already put the children in their beds, heard their prayers, which I might add included thanks for the puppy, and looked in on Gran, so you won't need to do that. Want to sit on the patio for a while?"

"Maybe I'd better not. You need to rest."

"What makes you think I can't rest when you're around?"

He looked at the brochure she clutched in her hand, and she blushed. "I'm tired tonight, Mark. I didn't stay at the farm long after you left, and I've been plodding around battlefields for the past few hours."

Mark opened the door to her room, but he leaned against the doorjamb preventing her entrance. "Something has happened since I left you," he said. "Excuse me for prying, but what are you doing that your mother doesn't approve?"

"She thinks I should spend more time and money on my sister's children, rather than taking care of Kristin and Eddie." That was enough for him to know—she couldn't worry him with her mother's opinion of their relationship.

"I am sorry if your work here has caused a problem with your parents," Mark said.

"Oh, this started when we were children. Since I was the oldest child, Mom thought I should always sacrifice for Nancy. If I had a toy Nancy wanted, I had to give it to her. That sort of thing."

"You don't sound bitter about it."

She shook her head. "No, I've always loved Nancy, so I didn't mind. And I like her children, but helping them doesn't give me the satisfaction I receive taking care of your kids. It irritates me sometimes that Mom doesn't realize I have needs as well as Nancy." She laughed lightly. "I shouldn't be bothering you with my problems—you have enough of your own."

He touched her cheek. "I've unloaded my frustrations on you plenty of times, so I'm here to listen whenever you need to talk."

"Thanks, Mark. I'll be all right in the morning."

"Good night then, Alice. The kids were so excited coming home, and they couldn't wait to tell Gran all about it. Thanks."

She walked around him and entered her room quickly. He looked as if he wanted to kiss her, and she couldn't allow that.

The next evening, after dinner, Kristin and Eddie went into the backyard to play, and Mark tarried at the table after Gran went to her room. While Alice cleared the table and filled the dishwasher, Mark fiddled with his tea glass, and was unusually quiet, so Alice knew some problem was vexing him. When she turned on the dishwasher, Alice poured a cup of coffee and sat opposite Mark at the table.

"We should make a decision about when to get the puppy," she said, "and perhaps agree on rules to discuss with the kids, such as—does the puppy live in the house, or does he have a home in the backyard?"

"I've got a bigger problem on my mind tonight. I've decided to sell this house and move into a smaller, less expensive place. I talked to a loan officer at the bank today, and with the equity I've built up in this house, the payments on a smaller home would be in a range I could easily manage."

"Have you looked at smaller homes?"

"Yes—there are several nice houses on the market that I can afford to buy, but they're too small for us. Most of them are two or three bedrooms. It's more important now than ever that the children have their own rooms. I suppose Eddie and I could room together for the time being until I'm financially stable."

To Mark's credit, Alice knew he hadn't once considered any plans that didn't include Gran, who really wasn't his responsibility.

"We should never have bought this house. I know it now and I knew it at the time—we couldn't afford the high payments, but we could have made it if Clarice and Eddie hadn't gotten sick."

"You haven't closed any deal yet, I suppose."

"No—I won't make a decision until I talk it over with the children and try to explain to them why a move is necessary. I'm still hoping for a house with four bedrooms, even if the rooms are small.'' Most of the time he'd been talking, Mark had looked down at the glass he was twirling on the tabletop, but now he looked directly at Alice. ''What do you think about it?''

She smiled at him. ''There wouldn't be any place for a live-in nanny in a smaller home, and perhaps that's just as well.''

Emotion darkened his eyes, and instead of being blue as the sky, they darkened to the shade of a tranquil lake. ''I won't buy any house that doesn't have room for you.''

Her pulse quickened at this declaration, but she said, ''I can live in an apartment and come in during the day. In fact, after the remarks my mother made yesterday, I'm wondering if that isn't a good idea anyway.''

''Oh, so that's what upset you! That's the reason I haven't told you before we'll have to move. I was afraid that would be your reaction.''

''If this move will ease your burden, you shouldn't be concerned about me. I can come early in the morning, get the children off to school, and be here when they come home from school and stay until after dinner. We can manage all right.''

He shook his head. ''It may come to that, but it's the last alternative I'll consider.'' He smiled slightly. ''And what comments did your mother make?''

''Mom has always had a tendency to disagree with my decisions, which I could understand if I was still a girl. She says it isn't good for my reputation to be staying here. I told her that we're always well chaperoned and have never been in the house by ourselves, but she was unconvinced. I'm not concerned about her attitude—I've lived with it all of my life—but I do wonder if others share that same opinion.''

"Surely not! I wouldn't have considered a live-in nanny if Gran hadn't been here.''

"I suppose it wouldn't have bothered me, if I didn't have some guilt about the way I feel about you. The thing is, Mark, I don't want to be responsible for any hint of scandal about you. I pray daily that you'll return to the ministry God called you to. I don't believe you can be content until you take up the cross you promised to carry for Him. When that happens, I don't want anyone to question the nature of our relationship.''

He shook his head slowly, and rubbed his chin with his hand. "You're right—I've been miserable since I accepted the position at the bank, which I thought would alleviate my financial problems, and not only have they gotten heavier, but my spiritual burden has, too. The only time I'm content is when I'm at home, and you know the reason for that.''

Suppressing a desire to circle the table and clasp him in comforting arms, Alice stayed remained seated, and she said, "I try to shield you from as many problems as I can, and—'' she smiled at him ''—you know the reason for that.'' She stood up and dumped the last of her coffee down the sink. "It's time for us to talk about a less sensitive subject—what about the dog?''

Mark shook his head stubbornly. "I'm not ready to talk about the dog yet.'' She leaned back against the sink cabinet. "Right now, I have to put the welfare and security of Kristin and Eddie before my own happiness. You do understand that?''

"Of course—you don't have to say anything more."

"I can never say all the things I want to say, but hear me out this once. I can't plan very far into the future yet, but in a few months I hope my situation has improved until I can talk about us. When that time comes, will you listen?"

"Yes, Mark, but until then I'm only the nanny, and we both have to remember that. There's a scripture verse that you know better than I, but it's the key to the way we must approach our relationship. 'If our hearts do not condemn us, we have confidence before God and receive from him anything we ask, because we obey his commands and do what pleases him.' As long as we haven't done anything wrong, I'll try not to worry much about others. I just want our consciences clear."

A weary sigh escaped his lips. "I agree. Now what's this about a dog?"

"No matter where you live, we've promised the kids a dog."

"What do you want to do with it?"

"Keep him in the utility room for a few weeks, and then take the dog to a house in the yard. Those pups are basset hounds, and hardy animals, so it isn't necessary for him to stay inside."

"Suits me."

"And another thing, I have access to a beach house on a private strip of land north of Virginia Beach. Will you let me take the kids and Gran down there for a week before school starts? It wouldn't cost you anything. It would be a great opportunity for them, but I worry about leaving you alone."

"Gran probably won't go."

"I'm not so sure—she was very lonely while we were at the farm."

"I'd miss you, but I don't want to prevent the children from having some fun. They've never had the opportunity to do these things—with Eddie and Clarice both being sick, we never had a family vacation."

"Do you have any vacation coming?"

"My boss told me to take off a few days. I could probably come down for part of the time you're at the beach."

"Oh, that would be great, Mark. The kids would love it."

He got up from the table and towering over her, he gave her a quick hug. Smiling, he said, "As if the two of us won't also."

"Then I'll make arrangements about our housing, and we should get the puppy before we leave. The children and I can pick out a dog house tomorrow, and go after the pup in a few days."

The next afternoon Erin invited Kristin and Eddie over to play. While waiting for the washer repairman, Alice had some free time. With some misgiving, Alice went into Mark's home office. The desk wasn't locked, and being careful not to leave any evidence of her searching, she found a file containing the record of what Mark owed on the house and where the loan was held. She jotted down this information and other facts she thought would be needed and replaced the file in the desk.

The repairman finished an hour before she was to pick up Kristin and Eddie, so Alice drove to a booth in a shopping center and telephoned her accountant, Melvin Haycraft. He'd been John's financial advisor for years, and Alice had an amiable working association with him. He'd often complimented Alice on her business decisions, but he was leery of her present proposal.

"I want you to anonymously make some payments on Mark Tanner's house. I have information that will help you look into it. I'll need your advice on the best way to do it."

Alice read the information she'd taken from the file in Mark's desk.

"You know there's a limit to the amount of money you can give away in a year."

"I know that, but I'm sure you can find a loophole if need be."

"Who is this Mark Tanner? A relative of yours?"

"I told you I'd taken a nanny position. Mark Tanner is my employer—I take care of his children, and if he doesn't get some help, he's going to lose his house. I don't expect to pay all of the debt, but I want to assume enough to give him the boost he needs. You find out how much that will amount to, and I'll put my request in writing. Above all, I don't want *anyone* to know where the money comes from, and it has to be done as soon as possible."

"Well, I'll do it, but against my better judgment. And for goodness sakes, don't give away any more money. You've given your sister and parents too much already. You have a secure investment, but you can't keep it secure by giving away thousands of dollars on a whim."

"It isn't exactly a whim. I'll telephone you again in a few days. Don't try to contact me."

Two days later, Alice took the children to the farm to choose the pup. She'd expected a quarrel as to which dog they'd take, but they both preferred the runt of the litter, an almost white male with long brown ears and a few soft brown spots on his soft hair. The mature dog would eventually have some black patches of hair. She'd brought a box from the house to transport the animal, and he did a lot of whining and clawing as they drove down the highway.

While they'd agreed on the pup they wanted, Kristin and Eddie bickered most of the way home over the name of their pet.

"Each of you write down the names you prefer, and we'll put those names in a box and have your daddy draw out a name when he comes home tonight. Is that fair enough?"

"But, Alice, I can't write," Eddie protested.

Laughing, she said, "I'd forgotten that little detail. When we get home, you can whisper to me the names you like, and I'll write them down for you."

"Are you going to make him sleep out in the yard tonight?" Kristin asked.

"He can stay in the utility room for a week or so at night, but he does need to be out there during the day. We'll stop at the pet store and buy some food, and then you and your father can decide on your duties in caring for the dog."

As soon as he walked in the door, the two children rushed at Mark. "You have to draw out the name, so we'll know what to call the puppy," Kristin shouted. "Hurry."

Eddie picked up the box from the kitchen table. Mark closed his eyes, stirred the pieces of paper, and drew out one.

"What is it?" Eddie asked.

Mark spread the paper on the table. "Buffy," he said.

"That's the name I chose," Kristin said.

"I did, too, didn't I, Alice? You know that's the name I wanted."

"That's a relief," Alice said in an aside to Mark. "Then both of you should be happy. Buffy, it is."

The children pulled at Mark's hands to take him into the backyard to see Buffy, while Alice made last-minute preparations for their meal and called to Gran that the food was almost ready.

"Dr. Zane's receptionist telephoned today to remind you that Eddie has a checkup next Tuesday afternoon." Alice said when they sat down for dinner.

"I knew it was coming up soon. We wanted the exam before he starts to kindergarten."

"Shall I take him?"

"I'll arrange to take an hour or two off from work, but I do want you to go with us to hear the doctor's diagnosis."

"I'll bring Eddie down to the office, and we can go from there—that will save you the time coming out here after us."

When Alice set out with Eddie for the appointment, he looked little and forlorn in the car seat.

"There's nothing to be afraid of, Eddie. This is just a routine checkup, and I'm sure the doctor is going to be pleased with how you've grown this summer. I'll tell you what, I'll give you a dollar for every pound you've gained."

Even the promise of money didn't encourage Eddie much.

"But what if he says I can't go to kindergarten? That's what Ethel said would happen."

Although Ethel's visits weren't as frequent, she still dropped in once or twice a week, and Alice didn't monitor what went on when she was with the children. As long as Mark didn't object to Ethel's visits, what could she do?

"I doubt that. So don't worry about it."

"A dollar for every pound, Alice?"

"That's right."

"But what if I've gained ten pounds?"

"Then you'll have a nice ten-dollar bill to spend any way you want to. What would you like to buy?" she asked, pleased she'd gotten his mind off the outcome of the doctor's exam for the moment. Eddie was still mentioning items he would like to buy when they arrived at the bank's parking lot, where Mark was already waiting in his station wagon.

"Alice is going to give me a dollar for every pound I've gained," Eddie announced as soon as they transferred from the van to Mark's vehicle.

Mark frowned at her, and she shuddered inwardly to consider his reaction if he found out she was reducing his house loan.

"Eddie is jittery about this trip to the doctor because Ethel told him he wasn't well enough to go to kindergarten. He needed something to keep his mind off the exam."

"I'll admit it's a good idea, but I'm already so much in your debt, I'll never be able to repay you."

"When you give someone a gift, it doesn't have to be repaid. You don't owe me anything, Mark."

Had she been wrong to pay on his house loan without asking him?

When they reached the waiting room, instead of sitting with his father, Eddie sat on the chair next to Alice's and snuggled against her. She noticed frequently that while Kristin wanted to be by Mark's side all of the time, Eddie depended more on Alice than he did his father. Was this because the child missed a mother's love? No doubt he could barely remember when Clarice was physically able to mother him. If Mark had noticed Eddie's affinity for Alice, he hadn't mentioned it.

Alice picked up a book from the nearby table. It was a book about farm animals. "Let's see what you learned about the animals we saw at the farm. Do you recognize any of these words?"

Eddie soon became engrossed in the pictures and captions, completely relaxed when his name was called, but he held Alice's hand when they went down the hallway to Dr. Zane's office.

"Doctor," Mark introduced them, "this is Alice Larkin, the children's nanny. I wanted her to hear your report on Eddie."

Dr. Zane, a stalwart man in his forties, shook hands with Alice. "I've talked with Mrs. Larkin over the phone." He turned to Eddie. "And who's this strapping young fellow you've brought with you today?"

"I'm Eddie Tanner—you know me."

The doctor laughed and lifted Eddie to the examination bench. "Well, you could have fooled me— all brown and brawny. You look great, Eddie. What have you been doing?"

"We've been to Alice's farm—I rode the pony,

drove the tractor and played with the puppies. And Alice let us bring one of the puppies home." The doctor's glance shifted to Alice, a speculative expression in his eyes. "We take walks every day, too, and before school starts, we're going to the beach." A cloud filtered across Eddie's eyes. "Are you going to let me go to school?"

"I don't see why not. If a boy can drive a tractor, he ought to make it through kindergarten."

The doctor examined Eddie thoroughly and sent him for several X-rays. While they waited for the results of the tests, Mark suggested, "Let's go to the coffee shop for a snack. I'm anxious about the tests, and I'll get fidgety if we just sit and wait."

Mark had a doughnut and coffee, Alice ordered cola and Eddie wanted ice cream.

"I've cleared it with my boss," Mark said, "and I'll come to the beach for a few days."

"That's good, Daddy. You can play with me in the ocean."

"It will be more enjoyable for all of us if you're there, Mark." Alice's eyes conveyed more of a message than her words. "It will be good for you, too— even a couple of nights at the farm was relaxing for you."

"As soon as we return from the beach, we'll need to buy school clothes," he said.

"Do you want me to take care of it or will you go along when we shop?"

"You can buy some things if you'd like, but I want to go with you if we can find a good time— perhaps we can shop on Saturdays or in the evenings? There I go again, monopolizing your weekends and evenings! Forgive me, Alice."

"Do you think I'm unhappy at the way things are going?"

"You don't seem to be."

"Alice likes to look after us, don't you?" Eddie said, as he licked the last spoonful of ice cream from his dish. "You, too, Daddy—she tries to fix food you like, and when Kristin and me start fighting, she says, 'Stop this quarreling before your father comes home—I don't want you to worry him.' She likes you, Daddy."

Alice's face flushed. How much longer could she keep up this pretense of being a nanny in the Tanner home? She loved Mark and his children—and she wanted to be so much more to them than a nanny. She must go and visit Betty soon and let Betty's caustic remarks cause her to face the true facts.

No doubt, aware of Alice's discomfiture, Mark devoted his attention to Eddie, and didn't look at her. "It's a good thing for us that she does like the Tanners, Son." He wiped Eddie's face with a napkin. "Let's go see what Dr. Zane says about you."

Dr. Zane's face was beaming when he received them in his office. "The news couldn't be better, Mark. We've been through so much together with Eddie, that I rejoice with you. He's gained nine pounds in the past year, and while he still isn't as big as a boy his age should be, that's a vast improvement over his previous record."

Eddie's eyes sparkled at Alice, as if to remind her of the nine dollars she owed him.

"That's the best news you could have given me," Mark said, and his blue eyes were misty. "The majority of the credit goes to Alice—she's done wonders with the children since she's been with us."

Dr. Zane turned to Alice. "Whatever you've been doing—keep it up. Apparently you're the antidote that Eddie needs."

"So Eddie can start to school?" Mark asked.

"Yes, of course. You do need to realize that even though his heart problem is completely cured, he will be subject to other diseases. Because of Eddie's long illness, his constitution is weak, and he may contact minor bugs more easily than other children. You'll need to watch him closely."

"Doctor," Alice said, "we've discussed enrolling the children in riding lessons this fall. I assume that will be beneficial to them."

"Yes, and keep up the daily walks. Don't take Eddie out in extremely cold weather, for we don't want any respiratory problems, but he's doing great."

Chapter Seven

When they left Mark at the bank, Alice handed Eddie a five-dollar bill and four ones. "Do you want to spend some of the money before we go home? It might be a good idea to buy something for Kristin, too."

Alice stopped at a used bookstore, where Eddie chose a book on dinosaurs for himself, and a book about figure skating for his sister. When they got home, Alice said, "Let's have a celebration for Eddie's good report. If you kids will help, we'll set the table in the dining room for dinner, have candles on the table and everything."

Alice had discovered that Clarice had a beautiful set of English china, elegant crystal and sterling silver flatware. With some hesitancy, after she carefully washed the items she wanted for the table, while she shined the silver, she allowed Eddie and Kristin to dry the dishes and place them on the table, which she'd covered with a white polyester cloth. This resulted in having the napkins and silverware slightly askew, but the table did look festive.

She baked chicken breasts, cooked rice, green limas and prepared a salad. She still had time to bake a pie, and she made a chocolate cream pie—knowing that chocolate was Eddie's favorite flavor. The ice cream he'd had for lunch had been low-cal, so he could have a treat tonight.

Eddie and Kristin waited in the foyer for Mark, and they pounced on him as soon as he arrived.

"Come see the dining room, Daddy—we're celebrating Eddie's good report. It was Alice's idea."

Alice's happiness was complete when they sat at the table, en famille, and Mark said, with an apologetic cough, "Let's join hands and have a blessing before we eat.

"Dear Lord," he said, after a few false starts, "We have much to thank You for tonight. We always have had, but sometimes we failed to realize it. We're grateful for Eddie's good report today, thank You for Kristin, who's all a man could want in a daughter, thanks for Gran and her encouraging presence with us, and God, thank you for Alice. Guide us in Your love. Amen."

It was a festive occasion, with Eddie excited because he could start school, but so much attention was being paid to Eddie, that Kristin seemed unusually quiet. Alice had always suspected that she'd been neglected by her parents during Eddie's serious illness.

Trying to think of a way to give the girl some attention, she said, "Say, Kristin, I just had a thought. Would you like to have a sleepover for some of your friends before we go to the beach?"

"I've never had a sleepover," she said, but her face brightened. "When Mama was sick, Daddy didn't want me to."

"And that was right, too, but there's no reason you can't have your friends in for overnight now, if you'd like to. Okay, Mark?"

"That'll be fine. I suppose Eddie and I can survive one night with the house full of girls. How about it, Eddie?"

His mouth was full of chicken, but Eddie nodded his head in agreement.

"Then that's settled. Decide upon the ones you'd like to invite, Kristin, and I'll call their mothers after we agree on a date," Alice said.

"Is it all right if I tell Susie tonight?"

"Of course." Alice pushed back her chair. "If you want to help clear the table and carry everything into the kitchen, I'll take care of the rest of the work. I'm going to wash the crystal and china by hand—I don't want to trust it to the dishwasher."

"I'll dry for you," Mark said. "The crystal and china belonged to Clarice's mother, and it will be Kristin's someday."

"Then we'll be very careful with them. Perhaps I shouldn't have used it tonight, but I wanted it to be a special evening."

"It has been special, and a good time to use our fancy things. We've always used them when we had a celebration."

The children carried in a few items, and then headed for the family room—Eddie to watch television, and Kristin to telephone her friend. Gran wended her way slowly and painfully up the stairs, and Alice watched her slow progress.

"I don't know how much longer she can manage those steps. She should have a bedroom downstairs."

"When she came here, I offered to move my office and let her have that room. It isn't much smaller than her bedroom, but she refused, thinking it was better for her to exercise by climbing the steps a few times each day. When we move, I'll try to find a house with a downstairs bedroom."

"Have you done anything more about that yet?"

"No, the loan officer is checking my options, but I haven't had time to look at any more houses. The bank pays me well, and in return, the officers expect a lot of work from me, but I'm not complaining."

As they worked companionably, Alice realized how much like man and wife they were, and she wondered if Mark was conscious of the same thing. Oh, if it could be! She believed that both she and Mark were ready for marriage, and that they would make a compatible couple. But what about the children—they accepted her readily as a nanny, but would they want her to take their mother's place? And Gran—how would she react if Mark took another wife? How long would she expect him to be faithful to Clarice's memory?

"Thanks, Mark," she said as she took the dish towel from him and hung it to dry.

"Thank you for all you do for us—the celebration dinner, Kristin's sleepover. You're giving us a home life that we've not had for a long time."

He stood too close for her comfort, and Alice replied lightly, "All in a day's work—for a nanny."

"Have it your own way, but you go way beyond what any nanny is expected to do, and I do appreciate it." He put his arm around her shoulders and gave her a brotherly hug, then his hands fell helplessly to his side.

"I feel so inadequate to—" His words were interrupted when Eddie called, "Daddy, come and read to me out of my new book."

Mark shrugged his shoulders. "See what I mean. Maybe the two of us can go out for dinner some night—just so we can have a little time alone," he said lowly.

Alice shook her head. "No, Mark—it isn't wise."

"I know that, but it's so frustrating at times. At least, don't shut me out of your life completely. When you go to your room in the evening and shut the door, it seems as if you're building a wall between us."

"The wall is already there—we have to accept it. Right now, Eddie and Kristin need all the security you can give them. I'm with them all day, and they need their father's influence at night."

"Daddy," Eddie called.

Mark started down the hall. "We used to sit on the patio and talk."

She shook her head. "We have to be cautious. Our situation is all right now, but I can't handle much more 'togetherness.'"

The sleepover was set for the Thursday night before they left for the beach on Saturday. Kristin invited five girls. When she gave Alice their names, Alice put in a call to the parents. All the invitations were accepted.

"Could we have a cookout? And what about renting some videos? Eddie will want to stay in the family room with us, but I don't want him. Little brothers can be a pest.''

"I wouldn't know—I've never had a brother—but I'll keep Eddie occupied. I'll rent a game for him to play on my computer."

"He and Daddy can watch television in Eddie's room."

Alice had noticed that Kristin was jealous of the time Eddie spent in her room. "That can be an option, but we'll look out for Eddie, so he won't crash your party."

Mark's homecoming was always the same. He'd enter the house and greet his children, who were usually in the family room, or sometimes in the foyer watching for him. Then, he'd come down the hallway to where Alice was busy in the kitchen. If she'd been his wife, he would have kissed her after a long day's absence, but as a nanny, all she received was, "Hello. How's your day been?"

On the night before Kristin's party, she sensed a difference in him—an excitement—indicated by his rapid steps and his brief greeting to his children. Usually he leaned against the doorjamb of the kitchen, his tie and coat held in his hand. This night, he came into the kitchen where Alice was removing a meat-and-vegetable casserole from the oven. After he closed the oven door for her, he said quietly, "The most amazing thing happened today! I'm still in shock."

Alice's hands moistened as she set the casserole on the kitchen table. Inwardly nervous, she smiled encouragingly. "Good news, I hope."

"Wonderful. Somebody anonymously paid thirty thousand dollars on my house loan today."

"That *is* good news, Mark."

"The best. I tried to find out where the money came from, but the bank officials don't know. It was handled secretively, but they've verified the authenticity of the loan, so it isn't a hoax." He sat down at the table. "You can't imagine what a relief it is to me. I feel like a bum taking the money, and if I knew who did it, I'd refuse. I'm assuming that it's one of my former parishioners, but there's no way for me to find out."

"I'm sure whoever donated the money wanted to do it anonymously or it wouldn't have been handled in this way. Just enjoy it, Mark. That's the only return your benefactor would want. Will this make a difference in your plans to move?"

"Oh, yes. If I have several months' grace on my house loan, I won't have any difficulty paying the rest of my bills, and I can do repairs around here that need to be done. It's wonderful to know that those debts have been canceled."

"Does this person's generosity remind you of a spiritual application?"

He smiled. "It reminded me of a sermon text I often used. I like to preach from the Old Testament, and I referred often to a passage from the book of Joshua when I wanted to stress the grace of God, and how we could do nothing to deserve it. 'I gave you a land on which you did not toil and cities you did not build; and you live in them and eat from vineyards and olive groves that you did not plant.'"

He paused thoughtfully, and Alice said, "That's a favorite verse of mine, too." She often thought of the words when she reaped the benefits of John Larkin's wealth.

"I'm not trying to justify myself for forsaking my vows to God," Mark continued, "but my life has been in such an emotional turmoil that I couldn't face people from a pulpit. I needed help more than others, and I felt like a hypocrite to preach on how to trust God for all your needs when I couldn't follow my own advice. I almost stopped praying, but one day I cried out in despair, 'God, I've given up—I don't know which way to turn. Send me a sign that You still love me.'"

Alice's hand gripped the chair back in front of her. One of the things she'd prayed for was coming to pass. Mark's hardened heart was opening to the leading of the Spirit.

"The day I prayed that, He sent you, Alice, and everything has improved since you came." He waved his arm to encompass the house. "This place that was almost like a tomb for a couple of years has become a home again. My children are happy. I look forward to coming home in the evening, when before, I dreaded to walk through the door. Although I've thanked God for sending you to us, I can't thank you the way I want to, but consider yourself kissed."

After she went to bed, Alice couldn't sleep, wondering if she'd made the right decisions about helping Mark financially. Was she putting him under such an obligation to her that he'd feel obliged to marry her, whether he wanted to or not? Would she be accused of buying a family? Could she keep her benevolence to Mark a secret? She felt as if she'd boxed herself into a corner without any means of escape.

For the sleepover, Kristin requested some special cookies that Alice had often made for the Tanner family, but she left the rest of the menu up to Alice. Since Alice had often attended parties for her sister's children, she knew what to prepare to make the girls happy. She cooked low-fat hamburgers and hot dogs on the grill, to be served with vegetable sticks, mixed fresh fruit, and coconut cream pie. For a snack, while they watched videos, she made a mixture of granola, dried fruit and nuts, and she had a good supply of fruit juices in the refrigerator.

Gran requested a tray in her room, and Mark carried it up while the others ate at the picnic table in the backyard. When the guests finished, Mark helped Alice bring the utensils and extra food into the kitchen, and left the girls to entertain themselves with active games and playing with Buffy. Alice put a video about the Creation into her television for Eddie to watch while she straightened the kitchen and made advance preparations for the girls' breakfast. Alice had rented a game for Eddie to play on the computer and she showed him how to operate it when the video ended. It was entertaining as well as educational. While they were still at the computer, Mark came to the door holding the newspaper in his hand.

"I can't find a place that isn't overrun by girls. May I join you?"

With a smile, so he'd know she was joking, Alice said, "Have you tried your office?"

"Yes, but it reminds me of the work I have to do. Besides, it's lonely in there."

"You're welcome to join us. Take the rocking chair—I believe it came from your room anyway."

When Eddie progressed until he could handle the

game by himself, Alice sat down on the bed and picked up her embroidery.

"Don't you want to sit here? I feel mean to take the only chair you have. We haven't made you very comfortable." Mark looked around the room with distaste. "And there isn't any heat out here. Some other arrangements will have to be made before winter." When she didn't answer, he said, "What're you doing?"

"Embroidering a tablecloth for my sister. I hope to have it finished before Christmas."

"My mother does a lot of needlework, and so did Gran before she had the stroke," Mark said.

"I didn't know that. I'm sure Gran is lonely, and I've been trying to think of something she could do to occupy her time. The next time I go to a fabric store, I'll look around and find an easy sewing project for her. Maybe I can find some items she can make for the children."

"She would like that."

His tender gaze flustered Alice, and she turned her attention to the embroidery.

"Is your mother still angry at you for coming to work here?"

"I shouldn't have told you that. Please don't worry about it. Mom irritates me at times, but I soon get over it."

"How old are your sister's children?"

"They're teenagers now, and quite a handful for their mother. Nancy worries that her ex-husband might entice them to live with him. I try to encourage her all I can—that's why I'm making this tablecloth. She loves handmade things, but she's never been good with needlework."

"Do you want to play the computer game, Daddy?" Eddie asked.

"Not tonight, Eddie. It's time for you to go to bed, and if I can find some earplugs to keep out the giggling and girl talk, I'm going to bed, too."

Eddie slid off the chair and came to Alice. He threw his arms around her neck and kissed her. "Thanks for letting me use your computer. Good night." He looked at Mark. "You gonna kiss her good-night, too, Daddy?"

Mark grinned. "Might as well," he said, and leaned over and kissed Alice on the forehead. For a moment their eyes connected warmly, and he was the first to turn away. "Don't let the girls keep you awake all night, Alice. Thanks for planning the sleepover."

The day after Kristin's sleepover, Alice went to see Betty.

Betty laughed when she entered the office. "Now, what's the problem? I may rue the day I ever sent you to the Tanners."

"I'm sorry to bother you so much, Betty, but you're the only one I can talk to about this. And don't think I'm sorry you talked me into being a nanny for the Tanners. It's an experience I wouldn't have missed, and you know why."

"And I'm not sorry either, for I've wanted you to know how wonderful it is to love that special man in your life. And why you're depressed about it, I can't imagine. Mark isn't going to mourn his wife forever—and if he doesn't fall in love with you, I'll be surprised. It seems a perfect setup to me. As their nanny, Mark and his kids have the opportunity to learn what a blessing you can be to them. It should be easy to move into the role of wife and mother.''

"But does it look like I'm ingratiating myself into their favor to trap him into marrying me?''

"I wasn't going to mention this to you, but Ethel Pennington is spreading a rumor that you're doing just that.''

"I'm not surprised—I don't know what Mark may have told her, but she seldom comes by the house anymore, and she would naturally blame me.''

"You see, the problem with Ethel is that she tried the very thing she's accused you of doing, and she thinks you're succeeding where she failed.''

"I'll admit I sometimes imagine myself as Mark's wife, but he'll be very hesitant about marrying again because his first priority is his children, and I can't blame him for that.''

"Don't you get along well with the kids? It seems that way to me.''

"I'm sure it wouldn't make any difference to Eddie because even now he clings to me more than to Mark, but I question how Kristin would take it. She's very possessive with her father.''

"Spiritually, how is Mark doing? I've noticed he's coming to church now.''

"He's seeking. He spends a lot of time reading the Scriptures, and he's having prayer at the dinner table. I've been praying for him to take up the cross he laid down.''

"You and hundreds of other concerned people! He's God's servant, and He won't allow Mark to wander much longer.''

"The main thing that's bothering me right now is that Mark has no idea about my financial situation, and I wonder how long I can keep him from knowing. Also, I feel deceitful not telling him, but it isn't very modest to say, 'I've got a lot of money.'"

Betty's eyes danced merrily. "I agree it isn't the best way to begin a conversation."

"Without going into detail, I've helped him quite a lot financially, but he doesn't know it. When I took the children to the farm, he accepted my comment that it was my childhood home and had no idea that I own the place. Next week, I'm going to take Gran and the kids down to my beach house. Mark will be there for a few days, and it's going to be difficult to keep him from knowing that I also own it."

"Do you still keep a housekeeper there?"

"Yes, Mrs. Guthrie has been in residence for several years, and she's very forthright. If nothing else, she and Gran will probably hit it off really well, and Gran will soon know my life's history."

"You shouldn't go to the beach."

"That may be true, but I want the children to have the opportunity, for I may sell the property before another season. The ill health of Eddie and Clarice kept them from ever having a family vacation. I've already made plans, so I can't back out now."

Betty looked at her for several minutes. "Am I to understand that you want advice from me?"

"I suppose so," Alice said with a grin, "as long as I don't have to take it."

"The longer you put off telling Mark that you're financially well-off, the more it'll irritate him. I'm surprised he hasn't already figured it out."

"He has so much on his mind that he hasn't given it any thought. I did tell him that I have an income from my husband—I just didn't tell him how much.

Now, I'm concerned about how he'll feel to know that he's obligated to me."

"I can't give you an answer to that, or even any advice. I feel that God's hand has been in this all the way—that you're what Mark needed to get back on his feet spiritually and financially. I'll be praying during the next few days that you'll come to some kind of an understanding with him. I want you and the Tanners to find happiness, and I fully believe that you can find it together. And, Alice," she added firmly, "there is such a thing as turning your worries over to God. You might try that."

Alice hadn't been home from Betty's office more than an hour when her sister, Nancy, telephoned. After they chatted for a few minutes about family affairs, Nancy came to the point of her call.

"Alice, I have the opportunity to buy a fabulous house. You know how we're cramped for space, and now that the children are older, it would be nice if they have their own bedrooms, and more space to entertain their friends. Can you let me have the money for the down payment?"

"How much do you need, Nancy?"

She named an amount near to the payment Alice had made on Mark's loan, and remembering what Mr. Haycraft had said, Alice's heart plummeted.

"Actually, Nancy, I can't help you now. A few weeks ago when I was talking to my accountant, he told me that I couldn't give away any more money this year. Some kind of federal regulation, he said. I could possibly help after the end of the year, but I can't promise for sure."

"But that's months away," Nancy wailed. "This house won't be on the market that long."

"But there might be another house available that you'll like even better. I can't do anything for you now. I don't have too much savvy about handling my finances—that's why I hire an accountant, and I follow his advice."

"You said you couldn't give away 'any more' money this year. What have you been doing with your money? You haven't given us much."

Not for the first time, Alice was sorry she'd inherited John's fortune. It had been a source of friction between her and her family, who seemed to resent every dime she gave to anyone except them, even the substantial amount Alice had donated to the community hospital in John's memory.

When Alice didn't answer her question, Nancy said, "Then you will help me buy a house after the first of the year?"

"I'll be willing to talk to you about it then—that's all I can promise."

Nancy's goodbye was hardly gracious, and Alice sighed as she replaced the phone receiver. Had she been justified in helping Mark's family only to refuse to help her sister? Betty's advice about trusting God with her worries popped into her mind.

Less than an hour passed before Alice's mother telephoned. Norma's voice was high-pitched, which Alice recognized as a sign of her anger.

"I can't believe that you'd actually refuse to help your sister buy that house," Norma said indignantly. "The way God has blessed you, why can't you be generous with your sister and her children?"

Alice didn't remind her mother how often she'd

been generous with her parents, as well as her sister, but it stung that they were so demanding and ungrateful. The Tanners, on the other hand, seemed to appreciate everything she did for them.

"Did Nancy explain why I can't help her right now? It isn't because I don't want to."

"What have you done with your money? Spent it all on the Tanners, I suppose. Alice, you haven't been the same since you went to work there."

Alice couldn't deny that, so she tried to change the subject. "How's Dad?" she asked.

"He's all right," Norma snapped. "You're avoiding the issue. Have you given any money to the Tanners? They should be paying you."

Tears stung Alice's eyes. She'd always given her parents the financial help they requested rather than to have any trouble. She wouldn't tell her mother to mind her own business, but she wasn't going to reveal what she'd done for Mark.

"Mom, I don't want to discuss this. I can't give Nancy any money now, so there's no use to talk about it. Did you have a nice family vacation at the beach?"

"It would have been better if I could have had both of my daughters there, but, no, you're taking care of your *new* family."

Norma terminated the telephone conversation without saying goodbye, and Alice prayed, "God, don't let me become resentful over my mother's attitude." But it did rankle that her parents and Nancy's family could enjoy two weeks at her beach house, free of charge, and not even be grateful for it.

Alice tried to put her despondency aside as she

helped Gran and the children pack the items they'd need for the beach.

"Now you're sure that I'll be all right, Alice?" Gran asked over and over. "I don't want to be a burden."

"Gran, there's a bedroom on the first floor for you, so you won't have to climb stairs as you do here. There's a boardwalk from the house to the water, and you can go down to the beach without trouble, or you can stay on the deck, watch the water and listen to the waves."

"It sounds like fun. I've always wanted to see the ocean."

"It's time you did, then. And you'll like the housekeeper, Mrs. Guthrie. She lives alone much of the time, and she'll enjoy having you for company."

"You say this is a family house?"

"No one except my family uses it," Alice evaded the question. "My parents and sister's family have just spent two weeks there."

The extra activities didn't lessen Alice's distress over the rift with her family, but she tried to prevent her poor spirits from dampening the enthusiasm of Gran and the children. She couldn't fool Mark so easily, and she felt his gaze upon her during dinner.

Before dark, they loaded their luggage in the van and station wagon, so they could get an early start the next morning. Buffy had submitted well to training, and since the two children had taken care of him, Alice agreed that they could take the pup with them to the beach. She went to the pet store and bought a carrier for Buffy, and she planned to haul the dog and his supplies in the van.

When Mark and Alice were alone for a few minutes, he said, "What's wrong, Alice?"

"I'm sorry you noticed. I'm having a little difficulty with my parents. I'll get over it soon."

He put his arm around her shoulders. "I'm sorry, Alice. When you're so warm and loving, I can't imagine why your family doesn't appreciate you as much as the Tanners do."

Alice leaned against him, and he tightened the embrace. How wonderful to have Mark's concern, even if she couldn't tell him the reason for the friction between her and the family!

"As long as the Tanners are on my side, I don't worry about anyone else. I'm glad you'll spend a few days with us at the beach," she said.

"I'll come home late tomorrow afternoon, but then I'll have the last four days of the week for vacation. I'm looking forward to having some time with you and the children, but I also need some time to think, and I want to be alone to do that."

"We have a private beach, and there are lots of places for solitude."

Gran rode to the beach with Alice, while Mark and the two children traveled in his station wagon. Alice made every effort to give Mark time alone with Kristin and Eddie, and this seemed a good opportunity for them to be together.

Gran dozed a good part of the way because she was in the habit of napping often, but when she roused, she took an interest in the scenery and proved to be a good conversationalist.

Once she said, "Have you ever considered marrying again, Alice?"

"I suppose every widow does," Alice said, "and my husband urged me to remarry. He didn't want me to live the rest of my life alone."

"Mark will probably marry again, but he was very devoted to Clarice, and he's still in mourning. I doubt he'll consider it until the children are grown. They wouldn't accept a stepmother very well."

"If that's the case," Alice said easily, "looks like I can stay on as a nanny for a long time."

With an effort, Alice endured Gran's reminiscences of the happier times of the family before Clarice had become ill. Were Gran's remarks deliberate? Had she sensed Alice's love for the family and was trying to warn her off?

When they pulled into a rest stop midway to the beach, Alice helped Gran into the rest room, and when they came out, Eddie and Kristin had already walked Buffy, he'd been restored to his carrier and the children were racing toward the playground.

"Do we have time for them to play a bit?" Mark asked. "They're getting fidgety in the car. We needed you to keep them entertained."

"We have plenty of time. It's only another fifty miles. I told Mrs. Guthrie we'd be there no later than five o'clock, so she knows what time to prepare dinner."

"Gran," Mark said, "do you want to sit in the shade, rather than to get back in the hot car? We won't stay very long."

"I'll sit on that nice bench over there. You go ahead and watch the kids."

As Alice and Mark moved toward the playground, she said in a low voice, "She's getting very tired.

At home, she spends a lot of her time in bed. I hope this isn't too strenuous for her."

"You continue to amaze me, Alice—not only do you take care of me and my kids, you're as good to Gran as if she were your own grandmother, rather than a stranger. Not many people would have included her in this trip. She'll be a lot of trouble for you."

"Oh, she'll spend most of her time with Mrs. Guthrie, who will enjoy having someone her own age."

"We haven't discussed the cost of this vacation, and we should. I don't expect to spend the week in your family's home without paying the expenses. Someone has to pay the upkeep of the place, and I can afford to pay for our room and board."

"The property belongs to me, and you're my guests."

He stopped abruptly and looked sharply at her. "I thought it was a family place—same as the farm."

Her eyes pleaded for understanding as she met his gaze. "Mark, I didn't like to deceive you, but I couldn't find any convenient time or place, nor even any reason, to tell you. My husband owned property, and when he died, I inherited it all. The farm's mine, too. John bought it so my folks would have the money to buy into the retirement home where they now live."

He moved on slowly toward the children. "I hardly know what to say—you've indicated that you had an income and didn't need what I'm paying you, but I didn't know to what extent."

"But *I* knew, Mark, and if I hadn't wanted to work for you, I wouldn't have come. Now that you know,

I hope it won't change our relationship. My life before I came to you has nothing to do with my nanny position."

"I suppose not, but I feel I'm getting further and further in your debt."

"This beach house is a liability, and my accountant has advised me to sell it, for the upkeep is expensive. Except for a few weeks in the winter when she goes to Florida, Mrs. Guthrie stays there all the time as caretaker, but she wants to retire. Since I probably won't own it next year, we might as well enjoy it before the children go back to school. Except for the food, it won't cost any more for us to be there than if the house stood empty."

"I can at least pay for the food."

"All right. When I check Mrs. Guthrie's food accounts, I'll tell you how much, but it isn't necessary."

While Mark played with the children, Alice sat on a bench and watched them. He'd taken the news of her wealth better than she'd thought he would.

Chapter Eight

When they left the rest stop, Alice took the lead since Mark didn't know the direction to her house. After they passed through the town of Virginia Beach, she traveled north until they reached a row of private homes fronting on the ocean. She turned into the driveway to her home, separated from the neighbors by a high board fence. The two-story frame house, its structure resembling the prow of a ship, was painted a soft brown. Decks extended along the front of the house at both levels. Floor-length windows afforded a full view of the ocean that lapped gracefully at the sandy beach. Shrubbery grew along a low seawall, and a boardwalk provided a convenient path to the beach. Benches stood along the seawall facing the ocean.

When Mark stopped behind her van, the children tumbled out of the vehicle and headed toward the ocean on a run. Alice released Buffy, and he chased after the children, falling all over himself in his excitement. Mark looked in wonder at the magnificence of the property.

"Kristin, Eddie," Alice called. "Stay out of the water until your daddy or I are with you."

"And this is yours?" Mark said, shaking his head in amazement. "I expected a cabin of some kind."

Mrs. Guthrie, a plump but energetic senior citizen, appeared in the doorway.

"Welcome," she called in her genial way. She came to the van and stuck her hand in the window. "You must be Gran Watson—I'm glad to have someone my own age around for company while the younger generation plays in the water. Need any help getting in the house?"

"Mark and I'll help her, Mrs. Guthrie." Alice introduced Mark to the housekeeper, who appraised him keenly, then looked quizzically at Alice.

Mark called for the children, and they were back from the beach before they moved Gran into the house. The children had stayed out of the water, but Buffy couldn't resist taking a swim.

"Buffy can't go in the house. Put him back in his carrier until we decide where he'll be staying," Mark directed Kristin and Mark.

"Gran will probably need to rest until dinnertime," Alice said, "so we'll take her to her room."

The inside of the house was spacious. Two bedrooms were located to the right of the entrance, with a living room and kitchen on the opposite side.

"Where are we going to sleep, Alice?" Kristin asked.

"Upstairs. There are three rooms on the second floor."

When Gran was settled, Alice and the three Tanners went upstairs. All the rooms had windows that looked out on the Atlantic. The largest room had twin beds, and one of the smaller rooms had a double bed, the other bunk beds.

"Can I have the room with the double bed?" Kristin asked.

"That's the one I intended for you," she said, "and Eddie and Mark can have the room with twin beds."

"Is this where you slept when you were a little girl?" Eddie asked.

"No, my husband bought this house a few years after we were married."

"He must have had a lot of money," Eddie said, wide-eyed.

"Not after he bought this property," Alice said with a laugh, and she glanced quickly at Mark, who refused to meet her eyes.

When Mark saw that she intended the room with the bunk beds for herself, he objected, "Alice, you shouldn't sleep in here. Kristin can take the smaller room," but when he saw Kristin's smile fade, he added, "Or Eddie and I can sleep in the bunk beds."

"Not at all," Alice said. "You're my guests—I want you to be comfortable. Let's bring up your luggage."

"Can we go swimming now, Daddy?" Kristin asked.

Mark looked at Alice, who checked her watch. "We have a couple of hours before Mrs. Guthrie will serve dinner. Why not?"

Mark said, "Come here, children, I want to talk to you." He squatted and put his arms around the kids and pulled them close. "I want you to promise me that you *will not* go to the oceanfront unless Alice or I are with you. I don't want to spoil your fun, but the ocean can be dangerous. Promise me?''

They both nodded solemnly, blue eyes serious.

''And after I go back to Richmond, I want your promise that you'll do exactly what Alice wants you to. We're in her home now, not ours, and I want you to behave like guests.''

Having extracted another promise from the children, they soon unloaded the vehicles and installed the luggage in the rooms. Buffy was housed in a small utility building behind the house.

''Are you gonna swim, Alice?'' Eddie asked.

''Yes. I'm on vacation, too. Mrs. Guthrie does all the work here. She won't let me help—she likes to spoil me.''

''Just like you do us?''

Alice ruffled Eddie's curls. ''I don't spoil you.'' Before she closed the door into her room to change into a swimsuit, she said, ''I put sunscreen in your rooms—don't forget to put a lot on. We don't want a sunburn to ruin your fun.''

''I'll look out for the kids while I'm here, Alice, so you can take a break.''

''Good enough.'' She changed into a swimsuit and put on a terry robe, a pair of sandals, and let her hair fall loosely over her shoulders. The Tanners were already playing in the water when she went down. She paused for a moment.

''I'm going to walk down the beach. There's about two miles of beachfront that's privately owned, but by reciprocal agreement, each home owner and guests have the privilege of walking along the water edge, but we swim on our own property. If you want to walk, that'll be fine. When you've finished playing in the water, there's a shower room back of the kitchen where you can wash off the salt water.''

Alice walked to the end of the private beach area, relishing the cool ocean breeze that blew through her hair. She stopped in front of the Hazard home, knowing that the Hazards were spending the summer in Europe, and that the house was closed. She spread her robe on the sand, applied sunscreen lavishly to her body, put on her sunglasses and lay down on the terry robe.

Her body relaxed, but her mind didn't, for she remembered the last time she'd come to the beach house. It was two years ago when John had finally accepted the fact that his illness was terminal. On the boardwalk that had been built for his convenience, she'd pushed him down to the beach in his wheelchair, and he'd been in an advisory mood.

"Alice," John had said, "we need to have a talk about what you'll do when I die."

After his illness, their marriage had developed into a daughter-father relationship.

"Oh, there's no need to think about that now," Alice had protested, wanting to avoid the inevitable as long as possible, for while she didn't have any romantic love for John, she did respect him highly. He'd been more influential in guiding her than her own father had been.

"You *must* give some consideration to what you'll do after I'm gone. When we return to Alexandria, I'll go over every aspect of my financial situation with you, so you'll understand it thoroughly, and I expect you to sit in with me on every appointment I have with my accountant from now on. Even before

I die, the doctors tell me that I may be incapable of handling my business affairs.''

And John had done that. Although he advised her to leave matters in the hands of the accountant he'd employed for several years, she understood John's financial status, and the last few months of his life she'd made decisions that he was unable to make.

After he'd finished discussing his finances, with the incoming tide coming closer to their feet, John had continued, ''And, Alice, I want you to remarry. You've been all that I've wanted in a wife, but I've always felt guilty that I asked you to marry me, and that I wouldn't give you a child, simply because I was too old to start parenting again.''

''It didn't matter, John.''

''You should have had children, for you would make a wonderful mother, but perhaps it still isn't too late. I can't live much longer, and I hope you'll find someone nearer your own age to love you.''

Alice didn't answer him, for she was sniffling, and John laid his hand on her bowed head. He hadn't mentioned the subject again, but it was good to know that she had John's blessing if she ever had the opportunity to marry Mark.

But if she did marry him—would she always have to take second place to his children? Would she become resentful of them? By the look in Mark's eyes when she started down the beach, she knew he wanted to go with her, but he had to stay with Kristin and Eddie, and while she approved that, still it gave her a lonesome feeling to know that the three of them were a mile down the coast having a good time, while she was lying on the sand alone.

Oh, stop feeling sorry for yourself, she chided herself, and turned over on her stomach and went to sleep.

Alice and Mark didn't have any time alone before he returned to Richmond the next day, but Mark insisted that Alice join him and the children as they spent the morning building a sand castle. Alice did so, but she believed that Kristin resented her presence. When Kristin and Eddie were alone with Alice, the girl was happy and carefree, but was it Alice's imagination that Kristin didn't want her to be around Mark? Perhaps the child sensed the attraction between them, and it wasn't surprising. When she and Mark were together, and especially if their hands touched, the emotional gravity was so powerful between them that Alice couldn't understand how anyone wouldn't detect it.

Mark may also have understood the problem Kristin was having, for he remained completely impersonal to Alice during the rest of the day, and she didn't even receive any of the mental messages that he often conveyed with his eyes.

After he left, Kristin joined Alice and Eddie when they walked along the beach, picking up shells and other treasures they wanted to take back to Richmond.

When bedtime came, Eddie said, "Now that Daddy's gone, you can sleep in my room."

Alice sat on the side of his bed and pulled him beside her. He'd just gotten out of the shower, and his hair was damp, his skin rosy, and he smelled of soap and shampoo. It was such a pleasure to feel flesh over his ribs and to know that he wasn't the skinny kid he had been.

"Sleeping in this room alone isn't any different

than when you sleep in your room at home. There's a light in the hall, and I'll leave my door open. You try to go to sleep, and if you get too afraid, I'll come in and sit on your bed until you are asleep. If a boy's big enough to go to kindergarten, he can sleep in a room alone.''

He nodded, his big blue eyes serious. "Okay, I'll do it. Daddy will be proud of me.''

"Your daddy is always proud of you whether you're a big boy or not, and so am I.'' Alice bent over and kissed his forehead.

Alice didn't hear anything out of either of the children all night, and she, too, slept soundly, but she awakened before daylight. Moving quietly, she put on a heavy robe and slippers, picked up her Bible, and went downstairs to sit on the deck. Facing the ocean, she saw morning dawn—the sun looked like a ball of fire as it slowly came into view over the horizon.

This had always been one of her favorite times at the beach. Alice turned in the Bible to Psalm 139, feeling as close to God as the psalmist must have been when he'd worshiped his Creator. "'Where can I go from Your Spirit? Where can I flee from your presence?... If I rise on the wings of the dawn, if I settle on the far side of the sea, even there Your hand will guide me, Your right hand will hold me fast.'"

The Bible lay open on her lap, but she read no more. Alice had never been more conscious of God's protective hand on her than she was right now. Since that day, when as a child, she'd accepted God as her heavenly father and Christ as her Savior, her life had been orchestrated by God. Ashamed that she sometimes had doubts about her future, she was thankful for moments such as this one when she praised God for the assurance that no matter where she was or under what circumstances, she was never out of the will of God.

She smelled coffee, so she knew that Mrs. Guthrie was out of bed. She wasn't surprised when the door opened behind her, and the housekeeper came out on the deck carrying two steaming cups of coffee.

"Couldn't sleep, huh?"

"Oh, I slept well," Alice said, "but I've had enough sleep." She sipped the hot coffee. "I'd forgotten how peaceful it is down here. I should have spent more time in this house, but my life has been in limbo since John died, and I haven't done much of anything."

"You're busy enough now."

Alice laughed lowly. "I don't have a spare minute, but I've never been so happy, either."

"You've adopted a nice family."

"They are nice, aren't they? I'm very fond of them, and when I have to leave their home, it will be heartbreaking. Betty St. Claire, head of the nanny agency, warned me of this when I took the job. I should have known better than to let my heart get involved with those two kids."

"Maybe you won't ever have to leave them," Mrs. Guthrie said, with an appraising look at Alice. "Are you sure your heart isn't involved with their father, too?"

Alice refrained from looking at Mrs. Guthrie. "My position in the Tanner home is as a nanny and housekeeper."

"I'm not exactly blind, you know. Besides, your

mother filled me in on the situation last week, so I was speculating before you came.''

"I should have known Mom would pressure you to advise me. She doesn't approve of my present position.''

"Oh, I'm on your side, no matter what you do. You and John have been mighty good to me.''

Alice reached over and squeezed Mrs. Guthrie's hand. "Thanks.''

"But I repeat—I don't see why you ever need to leave. From what Gran tells me, you're the homemaker and mother those kids have never had. She's hinted that her granddaughter wasn't too effective as a homemaker even before her illness.''

"I don't know—I've heard that, but I've never discussed Mark's marriage with him. I don't know what the future will bring, but right now, I'm the nanny.''

"If you say so.''

"I'm happy that you're visiting with Gran. She's quite alone in the world, and Mark should be commended for taking care of her.''

"I suggested that to her, but do you know, I've gotten the idea that she believes it's his obligation.''

When Mrs. Guthrie assured Alice that she could look after Gran and Buffy, Alice took the children to Virginia Beach on Tuesday. Mark had given Kristin and Eddie some spending money, but she added a twenty-dollar bill each so they could buy souvenirs that took their fancy. They spent a full day going in and out of shops, eating ice-cream bars and hot dogs, and enjoying all of the attractions. To the children's credit, they didn't spend all of the money on themselves—they bought gifts for Mark and Gran, and Kristin bought a gift for Susie, but when Alice asked Eddie if he'd like to buy a gift for Troy, he said, "No, I haven't forgotten the time he hit my belly with that ball."

His comment amused Alice, and she didn't remonstrate with Eddie then, but she decided that she would soon have to talk to him on the subject of forgiveness.

Mark telephoned that night, and Kristin took the upstairs extension while Eddie talked downstairs. They chattered to their father at least a half hour about their day's activities. Eddie finally handed Alice the phone. "Daddy wants to talk to you, too."

Alice's heart pounded when she answered. Just two days of not seeing Mark had been overlong.

"Hi, Mark," she said lightly. "I'm speaking on the downstairs phone. Kristin is still on the extension upstairs." She thought he should know that.

"Good night, Kristin—I'll see you Thursday afternoon."

"Good night, Daddy." Alice heard the upstairs phone replaced, and the extension light faded.

"Everything must be going well," Mark said. "The kids sound excited. But when are you going to have a vacation? You can't be a nanny all the time."

"We're having fun, and I am having a vacation. I haven't washed a dish, cooked a meal, or done any laundry since we arrived. We've been running around eating the wrong kinds of foods and wasting our money."

"Must be nice," he said, "while I've been working hard."

"In air-conditioned comfort?"

"Fortunately. It's hot here, and I'm looking forward to the weekend. I'm going to leave about noon on Thursday."

"There are several wildlife refuges in the area—I'd thought of taking Kristin and Eddie, but perhaps you'd like for us to wait until Friday, so you can go, too."

"I'd love that, but I do need some time by myself. I've been doing a lot of serious thinking about the future, and I feel that I can make some resolutions this weekend. I won't neglect the children, but I will try to get away for a while."

"They're sleeping late, and early morning is a good time to stroll along the beach and meditate. I get up early to sit on the deck and watch the sunrise. You can make a time for thinking."

"Please be praying about it, Alice—any decisions I make will involve all of us."

"I understand, Mark, and I've been praying for you, but it's hard to be specific in my petitions when I don't know what's best."

When Mark arrived on Thursday, he seemed at peace with himself, for his eyes were quiet and serene, and he was more relaxed than Alice had ever seen him. He'd gained several pounds during the summer, and he wore a pair of white shorts and a striped blue-and-white shirt. His outgoing personality and his good looks captivated Alice's heart all over again.

"You've got on a new shirt, Daddy," Kristin said.

"And new shorts, too. When I looked in my closet, I found I didn't have many sport clothes."

"We've been shopping, too," Kristin said. "Alice

took us to a big store, and we bought some school clothes.''

"She said you could pay her back later," Eddie added. "Come on upstairs and see our new things."

As Mark was ushered upstairs by his two children, he looked over his shoulder at Alice. "Let me know how much you spent," he said.

"I kept all of the bills."

The next morning, Alice heard Mark leave the house early, and he wasn't back by the time Mrs. Guthrie had breakfast ready.

"Where's Daddy?" Kristin demanded.

"Taking a walk along the beach."

Kristin jumped down from her chair. "I'm going to find him."

"Not until you've eaten breakfast. I think he'll be back by then."

Kristin pouted, but she did as Alice said, and Mark came into the kitchen before they'd finished eating.

"Am I too late for breakfast?"

Alice's eyes twinkled at him. "We do have rules about being on time for meals, but we'll excuse you this time."

They spent the morning at the wildlife refuge, enjoying the varied birds and animals in their natural habitats. During the afternoon while Mark and the kids played in the ocean, Alice visited with Mrs. Guthrie and Gran to give Mark some quality time alone with his children.

Saturday afternoon, when Kristin would have accompanied Mark on his walk, he said, "No, Kristin, I'd like to be alone for a few hours."

Kristin drooped in a chair on the deck.

"I could use some help getting ready for our picnic on the beach tonight," Alice said.

"I'll help," Eddie said. Kristin reluctantly agreed and she was soon over her disappointment, although Alice noticed that she frequently looked up and down the beach to see where her father was. He wasn't in sight, and Alice suspected that he'd stopped on the deck that the Hazards had built over the beach. She'd told him that the family was gone, and that he could have privacy there.

The three of them gathered driftwood and piled it together for a bonfire. They carried chairs and a folding table down to the beachfront, and Alice taught them how to cut forked sticks to use for roasting hot dogs.

"We're going to make a freezer of homemade ice cream, too."

"I'm glad you're not making us eat all health foods this week, Alice," Kristin said.

"The value of any diet is moderation. Hot dogs aren't bad for you unless you have them every meal. I was rather strict with you at first because most of your food was fat, starchy and sweet. As long as we eat plenty of fruits and vegetables, we can add in our favorite foods, too."

"It's been fun here at the beach," Kristin said. "I sorta hate to leave."

Alice felt the same way. Whatever Mark was deciding now was going to make a big difference in all their lives, and it was cowardly to want to remain separated from the rest of the world—a world, where there were no Ethel Penningtons, or others who took the wrong attitude about her nanny position.

"School will be fun, too," Alice tried to reassure them. "But it's going to be very quiet in the house with the two of you gone all day. I'll miss you."

Eddie threw his arms around Alice's legs—now that he was stronger, she had to brace herself for his gesture, so she wouldn't be thrown off her feet. "I'll miss you, too, Alice—maybe you can go to kindergarten with me."

"I doubt that—someone has to stay home to look after Gran and have a snack ready when you get back at the end of the day!"

Mark returned when they were almost ready for the picnic. He was relaxed, but Alice couldn't tell what he'd decided by his expression. His thick hair had been ruffled by the breeze, and several locks dangled over his forehead.

"Sorry I'm so late—I intended to help, but I went to sleep."

"We have everything ready, but you might want to push Gran's chair down here. She insisted that it was too much of a trek for her, but we convinced her otherwise. It's a beautiful, warm night, and she'll enjoy it."

"I'll bring her." He sniffed appreciatively at the pan of corn Mrs. Guthrie carried past him. "This sea air must whet my appetite. I'm hungry all the time."

After they'd eaten the hot dogs, roasted corn, fresh veggies and fruit, Mark hand-turned the ice-cream freezer, assisted by Alice and the two children. Mrs. Guthrie brought a bowl of fresh strawberries for topping.

It was growing dark by the time they finished eating, and Mark wheeled Gran back to the house. Mrs.

Guthrie stayed with them while they sang campfire songs, and waited for the moon to rise over the ocean.

When Mrs. Guthrie announced it was her bedtime, Mark said, "You kids need to go to bed, too. I'll take you to the house and get you settled in, and then I'll come back and help store the chairs and table."

Mrs. Guthrie said, "We can each take a load of things as we go, and there won't be much left to do."

Mark stepped close to Alice. "Wait here for me— we have to talk," he said quietly.

Alice had doused the fire and carried the rest of the chairs to the house when Mark returned. She saw the lights go out in the upstairs bedrooms, and she waited by the seawall until Mark came down the walk.

"Let's sit on this bench," she said. "The wind has picked up now, and we'll be more comfortable here."

"This is fine," he agreed, and sat down beside her. Mark took Alice's hand and caressed it gently. "I've decided to go back into the ministry, Alice."

Even though she'd expected the news, his words excited Alice, and she lifted her arms to embrace him, but she stopped abruptly and moved farther from him.

"That's wonderful. It's such a waste for a man like you to be away from the position God called him to fill. Are you at peace about it?"

"I've been fighting this decision for a year, although the struggle hasn't been as difficult in the past few weeks. This afternoon when I walked along the beach, I took a small book of poems by Francis Thompson. One of the poems, 'Hound of Heaven,' is Thompson's experience when he was out of the will of God. He, too, ran away from the life God wanted him to live. For years he tried to escape God, but like a hound pursuing his quarry, God stayed on his trail until the man finally submitted to the divine will for his life.''

"Yes, I've read the story," Alice said. "It's a beautiful illustration of how God intervenes in an individual's life."

"I've finally realized that God isn't going to release me from the vow I took, and I don't want Him to. I'll never be content—be fulfilled—unless I'm in a ministry of some kind."

"What is your next step?"

"I've started some projects at the bank that will take a few months to complete, and it wouldn't be ethical for me to resign right away. But I will contact the leaders in our state organization for advice and counseling. I may be called to the pastorate again, or perhaps I might be more effective as a counselor or chaplain. It doesn't really matter where I work. Now that I've turned my life over to God's leading, I'll follow Him wherever He leads."

"You're going to make many, many people happy, including me."

"I know," he said ruefully. "I've disappointed all my friends." He moved closer to her. "Now, I want you to do what you started to do when I told you my news."

"Oh, Mark," she whispered, as she snuggled into his arms and clasped her hands around his neck. "I've missed you so much this week."

"I can understand that. I could hardly bring myself to go home in the evening when I knew you weren't

going to be there. I ate most of my dinners in a restaurant.''

For a few minutes, she rested content in Mark's
embrace. The wind died down, and the waves gently
lapping on the sand complemented the rhythmic
thumping of their hearts. As close as they were, Alice
could feel Mark's steady heartbeat through the soft
fabric of her shirt.

"Now it's time to think about us." She stiffened
slightly in his arms, and he sensed it. "We have to
face it, Alice, so relax."

Alice knew he was right, but she wished they
could stay this way and avoid making further decisions, at least tonight.

"I love you, Alice, and it's been almost more than
I can bear to have you in my home as an employee
rather than my wife. I want to change that. If you
bring such contentment in our home when you're a
nanny, I can't imagine what it will be like when
you're the wife and mother. Will you marry me?"

"Of course, I'll marry you, but when?"

"The sooner the better, although we will have to
consider Kristin and Eddie. They both love you
now— I don't think they'll object."

"I'm not sure about Kristin—she's rather possessive toward you. For the kids' sake, we should wait
a few more months, although I want to marry you
now."

"You may be right, but if we marry right away,
that would settle any gossip about our relationship. I
thought with Gran and the children in the house, no
one would question your position, but apparently
Ethel suspects our mutual feelings, because she's
hinted as much to me.''

"Try as I might, I can't hide how much I love you. Betty knew right away, and my mother and Mrs. Guthrie have made comments. I'm surprised that Gran hasn't known it."

"I've never discussed my first marriage with you, and the least said the better, but both of us have had former mates, and we can't change that. I don't mean to be disloyal, but you mustn't think you're competing with a first love that I can't get over. I never felt for Clarice what I do for you. Never before have I experienced the excitement, satisfaction, and emotion that you've brought into my life. You won't be taking second place—you'll have the best that's in me to give."

Alice sniffled. "Mark, thanks for saying that. I'll never expect you to mention it again, but I've been feeling a little slighted—seems like you always choose your children before me. I know it has to be that way, but I'm glad you told me that I'm first with you in many ways. You know I didn't love John, so God has been good to us. Both of us know now what we missed in our first marriages—God must have intended for us to be together."

For a long time they sat in close embrace without speaking, until Mark finally said, "Are you asleep?"

"No, just content. I feel as if I could stay this way forever." She stirred in his arms and shivered a little. "We'd better go in. I doubt I'll sleep, but the children might awaken and want something."

She lifted her lips to be kissed, and Mark didn't disappoint her. "I love you, Alice," he whispered as his lips hovered over hers.

Holding hands, they turned toward the house. "That's strange," Alice said. The living room was fully lighted. "I thought everyone was in bed." She quickened her steps. "Can anything be wrong?"

Chapter Nine

Alice stepped into the house ahead of Mark to be confronted by Kristin and Gran, both staring belligerently at them.

"Kristin, I thought you were in bed asleep," Mark said. "It's too late for you to be up."

Kristin jumped out of her chair and came forward. "We saw you," she said, tears sparkling in her eyes. "You were kissing."

Mark squatted beside Kristin and tried to take her in his arms, but she jerked away from him.

"If we were ashamed of what we were doing, we wouldn't have been in full view of the house. You'll probably see us kissing quite often—we're going to be married."

"No," Kristin shouted. "You're already married—to my mother." She turned on Alice. "You're trying to steal our daddy away from us."

Had she heard this from Ethel? Alice wondered.

"At least you could have had the decency to wait a year or so," Gran said angrily. "You should honor the memory of my granddaughter, rather than take up with a servant in your house.''

Alice couldn't believe this scene was real. She would awaken soon and find it was all a dream. She sank into a chair, feeling like a traitor to leave Mark to deal with them alone, but she couldn't speak in her own defense.

Wearily, Mark said, ''I don't have to justify my actions to either of you, and I've said all I'm going to right now. Kristin, go to bed.''

Kristin sulkily turned toward the stairs, while Gran in her slow way guided the walker to her room. Mark turned off the overhead light, and plunged the room into semidarkness. From the light at the head of the stairs, Alice watched him as he stood in front of the window, looking out toward the ocean, with knotted hands jammed in his pockets. His body trembled violently, and Alice knew he struggled to control his anger.

At last, with an audible sigh, he sat on the floor beside her. She threaded her fingers through his wavy hair.

''I wish I could have spared you that tirade. When I think of the way you've sacrificed for all of us this summer, I can't believe they would actually say the things they did. You have absolutely no obligation to Gran, and you've included her in everything, took her to church, watched out for her health. And she called you a servant!''

''Forget it, Mark.''

''I'll never forget it. And Kristin—to think that a child of mine could be so disrespectful.''

''Both of them are insecure. Gran knows that you aren't obligated to give her a home, and if we marry, she probably thinks I'd expect her to leave, although I've never given her any reason to believe that. As for Kristin, I told you she's possessive with you—she doesn't want to share you with anyone.''

''Just like her mother,'' he mumbled, but Alice chose to overlook his remark.

''It's like you,'' he continued, ''to find excuses for them, but I can't be that benevolent yet. Right now, I feel like snatching you up in my arms, leaving all of them behind, and going away together.''

Alice bent over and kissed the top of his head. ''Not Eddie—I wouldn't leave him behind.''

He took her hand. ''Of course, I'm angry now and didn't mean what I said. I'm disappointed, too. Just when I thought my life was turned around and that the future was open before me, I have a problem rise in my own household. I don't know what to do about it.''

There was only one possible solution, but Alice wasn't going to mention it now—Mark had enough to worry him tonight.

''Think about a Scripture verse that I read during my morning devotions. 'In this world you will have trouble. But take heart! I have overcome the world.'''

''I've quoted that to members of my congregation who were experiencing trouble hundreds of times. Now my own words come back to convict me.'' He stood up and pulled her into his arms. ''I've been on a spiritual mountaintop all afternoon and evening, but now I've been plunged into the valley. Perhaps God needs to know how strong my commitment really is. But I've stood the test—my plans haven't changed at all. With you by my side, I can weather any storm.''

Alice wouldn't disillusion Mark, but as she lay awake most of the night, she could see only one solution to their problem. She wouldn't come between Mark and his family, and she didn't believe that Kristin would ever accept her. She kept telling herself that the Tanners could get along without her now—that her role in their life was to come and get them on their feet. Now that Mark was financially solvent and had made his commitment to return to the ministry, God wouldn't need her help in righting the Tanners' world. Did this mark the beginning of the end for her and Mark?

She faced the decision she'd dreaded all along. When it came time to leave Mark and his children, what would it do to her heart? If only she hadn't learned to love all of them, the break wouldn't have been so difficult. Tonight, she'd had a glimpse of paradise—of what marriage to Mark could mean. Had Moses felt the same way when God gave him a look into the Promised Land, and told him he couldn't enter? If it came to sacrificing her own happiness to make Mark's life easier, she'd do it, but she wasn't ready yet to give him up. She covered her head with the pillow and sobbed—hard, wrenching sobs that shook the bed. She couldn't control her sorrow—she only hoped that Mark wouldn't hear in his room across the hall, for she knew that he, too, would be unable to sleep.

Mrs. Guthrie looked from one to the other as they gathered for breakfast. Only Eddie was his normal self.

"I've had a good time here," he said, "but I want to get back to Richmond so I can go to school. Can we come back here again, Alice?"

"I don't know, Eddie. I'll probably sell the beach house before another summer."

"Aw, gee—I like it here." He sipped slowly on his orange juice and looked around the table. "Why's everybody so quiet?"

Mark glanced at Alice, but he shrugged his shoulders. "You and Mrs. Guthrie might as well know, Eddie—Alice and I've decided to get married, and Gran and Kristin are opposed to it. What do you think?"

Eddie's eyes lighted to a brilliant blue. "Oh, yes, Daddy. Get married. Alice loves me."

Alice bit her lips to keep back the sobs. Even Mark's eyes filled as he laid his hand on Eddie's shoulder. "She loves all of us, Son."

But Eddie's endorsement didn't have any influence on the opinions of Gran and Kristin. When Alice came downstairs with her final load of luggage, Gran was already in the back seat of the station wagon. Without speaking, Alice helped Mark pack both vehicles.

"Do you want Eddie to ride with you?" he asked.

She shook her head. "No, I'm just as well off alone. You go ahead—I'll need to talk with Mrs. Guthrie about closing down the house for the winter. She goes to visit her sister in Florida for a few months then."

"You are coming back, aren't you?" Mark asked anxiously, and she wondered if he sensed her struggle.

"Yes, I'll be there soon after you arrive, although I don't know what to say and do."

"We'll go on as we've been doing. Gran and Kristin will soon get used to the idea. It'll work out."

"I hope so."

The next few weeks were more disturbing than Alice had anticipated. Eddie didn't miss a meal, but Gran refused to come downstairs. She called an agency that delivered food to the elderly, and they brought her a meal once each day. The rest of the time she existed on food that Ethel Pennington brought her. Apparently Kristin had telephoned Ethel as soon as they returned to Richmond, for she came every day and took Kristin to her home. Alice had overheard several telephone calls Gran made to nursing homes indicating the older woman planned to move.

If Gran did leave the house, Alice would have to go even sooner than she expected, but she'd hoped to stay a couple of months for Eddie's sake. If she remained in the house without Gran living there, both hers and Mark's reputation would be ruined.

Kristin wouldn't let Alice take her to school, but asked Susie's mother to stop by for her each morning. Erin looked speculatively at Alice the first time she came, but Alice merely shrugged her shoulders—she couldn't talk about the tension in the house.

Mark was moody, as if a capricious streak had invaded his household, and he couldn't decide what to do about it. The only bright spot in Alice's life was Eddie. She'd taken him to school the first day and had spent a few hours with him as parents were expected to do. He was enthusiastic about his class and the new friends he made. He talked constantly when Alice picked him up and brought him home from school, and also during the evening meal, which he shared with her and Mark.

One evening when Mark came home, Alice sensed a difference in him—a new determination on his face.

"I see Ethel's car parked in front. Is she still here?" he asked.

"I suppose so. She never invades my part of the house."

"Will you come into the family room in a few minutes? I'm going to assemble the rest of the household, including Ethel."

She heard him going upstairs. "Kristin, Eddie," he called, "I want to see you in the family room. Gran, I'd like for you to sit in on the session, and you, too, Ethel."

They were all seated, expectantly, when Alice entered. She perched on a chair near the door. Mark stood by the fireplace.

"I'm returning to the ministry within the next few months," he announced.

"Oh, Mark," Ethel gushed, "that's wonderful news. I'm only sorry you can't come back to Tyler Memorial. Will you be so far away that your friends can't keep in touch with you?"

"I'm not prepared to say yet where I'll be, or what I'll be doing." He paused, and his eyes grazed everyone in the room before he continued. "For several days I've been wondering what to do about our family's situation, even questioning if I should accept the pastorate of a church when my own home is in such a turmoil. But I remembered when the Apostle Paul advised the church on what to expect from their pastors, he said, 'He must manage his own family well and see that his children obey him with proper respect. If anyone does not know how to manage his own family, how can he take care of God's church?'"

Alice became conscious of another quality that made Mark a good pastor. Always before she'd seen him as a counselor, a confidant, a servant to his people. Now he stood before them as dynamic as a prophet of old pointing out the sins of his people.

"So I've decided to manage mine. I've never been dictatorial with my family, but I am responsible for the upbringing of my children. In all honesty, I won't consider assuming the leadership of a church when I have an eight-year-old daughter who's rebelling against me and my personal decisions, even when she's being encouraged in this rebellion by adults."

The silence in the room was almost unbearable, and no one moved except Eddie, who crept out of his chair and scurried to Alice's side. She held out her hand and he leaned against her.

"Alice and I love each other, and I'm going to marry her in spite of what the rest of you think." He turned to Gran. "You can have a home with us as long as you like, whether it's in this house or in a parsonage someplace, but only if you accept Alice as my wife. If you don't choose to do that, you can leave."

Kristin was crying. "And, me, Daddy? What about me? Are you going to make me leave, too?"

He stared at her for several moments. "Of course, you can't leave. You're my daughter and my responsibility until you're of a legal age to make your own decisions. Even if you don't approve of Alice as my wife, you're expected to treat her respectfully as the woman I love.''

He surveyed Gran and Kristin with a stern glance. ''I just can't understand you two. Kristin, she's been the best mother you've ever...'' He paused and rephrased, ''The best mother you can hope to have. And, you, Gran, do you know of any other 'servant,' who would give you the love and attention you've had from Alice this summer? I'm out of patience with both of you.''

Finally, he turned to Ethel, and she took the offensive, shouting at him. ''How can you turn against your own family for a woman who took over your home as if she owned it and ingratiated herself with your children in an effort to trap a husband? Can't you see how she's manipulated you—put you in a position where you had no choice but to marry her?''

Mark held up his hand in protest, but Ethel refused to be silenced. ''She's been secretive about her past, but I did a little investigating. Alice is so stinking rich that she can buy any family she wanted—it was a sad day when she chose the Tanners.''

''A sad day for the Tanners or for you?'' Mark retorted, and his face was red with anger. ''Now I come to the part that I find most distasteful. I've never before asked anyone to leave our home, but I'm doing it now. Ethel, please leave and don't return, and—'' he turned to Kristin ''—you're not to have any further contact with Ethel. You'll be punished if I learn about it. Do you understand?''

Ethel's face blazed when she stood up. ''If she hadn't come here, you'd have married me. We were getting along all right before she showed up.''

Mark shook his head forcefully. "I'm sorry, Ethel—that isn't true. I had no thought of marrying anyone, especially you, but that changed when I met Alice. I firmly believe that God sent her to the Tanners to help us through the difficult days we've had."

Alice left the room—she couldn't bear anything more. Eddie followed her and Mark didn't try to stop them. She went to her room, sat on the bed, and Eddie cuddled beside her.

"Don't cry, Alice," he said. "Daddy loves you and so do I. Ethel's naughty to say those mean things about you."

Eddie's comforting manner brought tears to her eyes, but Alice swiped them away with the back of her hand. "I'm not going to cry. You help me set the table and get ready for dinner."

Wondering how many plates to put on the table, Alice gave Eddie five place settings, and he arranged them while she took a pan of baked fish from the oven and tested the potatoes to see if they were tender. Gran and Kristin came into the kitchen when Mark did, and took their regular places at the table. After he said the blessing, Mark grinned at Alice.

"You left before you got your orders. It will be a few months before we can be married, but in the meantime, you're to take your place as mistress of this home. No more going to your room until bedtime. You sit in the family room with the rest of us as if you belong there—as you do."

After she filled the dishwasher and laid out the items she would need for breakfast, Alice picked up her needlework and went to the family room, but she had little to say. Mark helped Kristin with her homework, while Eddie sat on the floor and played with some toy automobiles. When Eddie grew sleepy, and Mark was still busy with Kristin, Alice said, "I'll take Eddie to bed."

She was extra tender with Eddie as she rubbed his hair dry after he showered, and listened to his nightly prayers. When he got into bed, she lifted the sheet over his body, and kissed him. Even after Mark's ultimatum, she knew she must eventually leave. He could force Kristin and Gran to be civil to her, but you couldn't force love, and that was what she wanted and needed.

When she went downstairs, she paused at the door of the family room. "I'm going to bed, too. Good night, Mark, Kristin."

Kristin mumbled her reply, but Mark said, "No, I must talk with you, Alice. Come in for a few minutes."

She sat in an armchair and pretended to be reading a magazine while he finished with Kristin and took her upstairs to bed. When he returned to the room, he stood by the fireplace, his elbow on the mantel, and a muscle twitched in his face.

"Alice, I don't know why this hasn't occurred to me before, but Ethel's remarks about your wealth made me wonder. Are you the one who reduced the loan on this house?"

The crimson that flushed her face would have been answer enough, but she said, "Yes."

He threw up his hands and strode angrily around the room.

"I don't know why I didn't suspect that, since you had finally told me that you owned quite a lot of property, but to be able to pay out that much money to help a stranger must mean that you really *are* wealthy.''

"I hardly consider you a stranger, Mark."

"You know what I mean. My pride had suffered a lot this year—I suspected from the bountiful meals you prepared for us that you were spending more than I'd budgeted, and that you'd paid for Kristin's camp expenses, but I didn't want to make an issue of it. But this is the last straw! I won't take that money from you. I suppose that's the reason your parents have been angry with you—no doubt, they think I'm trying to get all your wealth, and if we're married, they, and probably everyone else, will think I'm marrying you for your money."

Alice had noticed that he'd said "if we're married." Did that mean he was having second thoughts?

"I'll go ahead and sell this house as I'd planned to and give back what you paid the bank."

Alice stood and, on trembling knees, walked to the door.

"Do whatever you want to, Mark," she said wearily.

Alice continued to live at the Tanners' although the tension in the house was almost unbearable. Mark wasn't the same, apparently still seething over the house payment, which he considered a loan, but wasn't able to pay back. If he intended to move to another location, he didn't mention it to Alice. In fact, they talked very little. Kristin and Gran didn't give her any trouble, but the happy family atmosphere was gone. Only Eddie remained unchanged, and she stayed on for his sake.

One event did bring some peace to her heart, for after a silence of two months, Alice's sister telephoned her one evening.

"I want to apologize," Nancy said immediately. "I know I shouldn't have been angry that you wouldn't help me buy that house. As it turned out, the house wasn't for me anyway. I've found a much better buy, which I can handle myself, and I signed the papers on it today."

Relief evident in her voice, Alice said, "I'm glad you let me know, Nancy. I'm sorry I couldn't help you, but it was impossible to do what you asked me at that time."

"I should have been grateful for what you've already done. I had a talk with Mom and Dad last night, and she's going to call you, too. How are things with you, Alice? Are the Tanners all right?"

Attempting to speak lightly, Alice said, "We have Eddie enrolled in kindergarten and that's a miracle in itself, considering all of the physical problems he's had."

Nancy chatted on about her children, and Alice was spared any further comments on her situation. She couldn't tell her family about her problems—she didn't want her mother saying, "I told you so."

When she confided her concerns to Betty, her friend advised, "Hang in, there. The man's pride has been wounded, but he'll get over it. Go ahead and marry him."

"He may have changed his mind now—he's so cool toward me."

The tension between Mark and Alice affected the whole house, and at the dinner table, the only time they were all together, Alice noticed that the children often glanced from her to Mark. She tried to act the same as she always had, but it was an effort, and the children were concerned. Kristin and Eddie helped her with the dishes, but as soon as the kitchen was in order, Alice went to her room. Eddie spent some time with her each evening, and he and Alice played games on the computer. Sometimes Kristin came, too, and while they played, Alice sat with her embroidery in her hands, but she made so many mistakes that she laid it aside. If she didn't have the tablecloth ready for Nancy's Christmas gift, she'd make it a birthday present.

One night, after Kristin had gone to bed, Eddie stood by Alice's chair. His lips quivered, and he said, "You're not happy like you used to be, Alice. Are you going away like my mommy did?"

"Eddie, the time will come when I *have* to go away. You'll be a big boy soon, and big boys don't need a nanny."

"I don't want you to go away, Alice. Don't you love us anymore?"

She hugged him tightly and buried her face in his soft curls. "I love you very much, Eddie. You're special to me."

"Do you love Daddy, too?"

Alice heard a movement at the door, and she looked up quickly and gasped. Mark leaned against the doorjamb, and she wondered how much he'd heard. She lifted a hand to her flaming face.

"Go ahead and answer his question, Alice," Mark said. "I'd like to hear the answer myself."

"Do you, Alice? Do you love Daddy?" Eddie

said. He turned a pitiful gaze on his father. "She's going to leave us like my mommy did."

Alice answered Eddie, but she didn't take her eyes from Mark's face. "Yes, I love your daddy, but I don't think he loves me."

Eddie ran to Mark's side, tugged on his hand, and pulled him toward Alice. "Tell her you love her, Daddy—I don't want Alice to go away."

A sob welled up from Alice's throat, and she covered her face in her hands. Eddie threw his little arms around her, and Mark knelt beside her chair.

"Son," Mark said, and his voice was tender, "it'll be better if Alice and I talk this over alone. Can you get ready for bed by yourself? I'll look in on you when I come upstairs."

Eddie stood on tiptoes and kissed Alice's cheek. "Sure, Daddy, just so you'll make Alice happy again."

As soon as they heard Eddie's steps on the stairs, Mark gathered Alice out of the rocking chair and carried her into the family room. He placed her on the couch, sat beside her, and held her close in his arms.

"Even if Eddie hadn't intervened, I can't stand this rift between us, Alice. Do you forgive me for being so foolish?"

Sniffing, she nodded against his shoulder, and moved closer in his embrace.

"I love you, but it's your money! You know that most ministers don't make big salaries, and I've never expected to become rich in the ministry—I've only wanted my needs met. My folks have worked hard all their lives and have accumulated very little. And I fall in love with a woman who can dole out money like she was Santa Claus! I don't see how we can ever have a happy marriage. I'll feel inferior all the time.''

Alice leaned back in his embrace and wiped the tears from her face. ''Until I married John Larkin, I didn't have any money, either. You've seen the farm where I lived until I went away to college. My folks didn't have the money or inclination to pay my way in college—I worked, took out student loans, and just barely scraped by. I did manage to pay all of my debts before I married John, so he didn't have to pay them.''

Mark threaded his long tapered fingers through his hair, and he stood up and walked around the room. ''Maybe I shouldn't ask—but how much are you worth? I'm going to marry you if you're as rich as Croceus, because I can't live without you, but I suppose I might as well hear the worst.''

''I really don't know. Besides the farm, which isn't worth a great deal, and the beach house, which is valuable, I own a home in Alexandria. My assets probably total a million dollars.''

Mark expelled his breath and dropped into a chair and groaned.

''That's worse than I thought.''

Alice went to him and perched on the arm of his chair. ''If my money is standing between us, I'll give it away. There are lots of worthwhile charities that will make good use of it. I'll live on what you can provide. It won't matter.'' She kissed the top of his head. ''Only one thing matters to me and that's you and your family.''

He shook his head. ''No, that isn't fair to you. I'll just learn to live with it.'' He lifted his head and put his arm around Alice. "But can't you understand how I feel and why I've been so undecided about what to do? For the past few years, I've been living from hand to mouth, and soon I'm going to be living off the largesse of John Larkin, a man I didn't even know. It doesn't seem right somehow."

"That's how I felt when I inherited the money, but my accountant set me straight on that. He said, 'In the first place, you earned the money—when you married John you gave him a new interest in life after Martha's death, and you took care of him during several years of illness. Besides, John wanted you to have the money, and he also wanted you to marry again.'"

"I doubt he'd want you to spend his money on another man and his family."

"That's where you're wrong." She told him then about the last day she and John had spent at the beach, and how he'd insisted that she marry someone her own age, whom she could love. "John was one of the most generous men I've ever known, and he was always interested in helping struggling pastors or seminary students. From what Betty has told me, you give yourself completely to your congregation. That's the reason you haven't succeeded financially—it isn't a priority for you, and that's how it should be. If you do return to the ministry, John would be overjoyed to know that his money is being used to support you and your family, so that you can do absolutely what God wants you to, and not have to worry about making a living."

Alice saw hope dawning in Mark's eyes. "He sounds like a wonderful man."

"He was. You see, his daughter had expected to

go into full- time Christian service, but her untimely death prevented that. I tell you he'd be happy I'm marrying you and making it easier for you to fulfil your vows to God.''

"You've eased my mind considerably, Alice, and I'll try to get over my qualms about your riches.'' He stood up and hugged her tightly. "I'm an ungrateful guy. Here I have you and a secure future for the taking, and I've made you and the family miserable for weeks.''

When he kissed her, time stood still for Alice. She whispered, "When can we get married?''

"Give me a little more time. I've written to the state board, asking for an appointment to discuss where and how I should continue. I'd really like to have that settled before we marry.''

"I'll wait, but I don't want to." She took a newspaper off the table. "In the meantime, would you be interested in buying another house? You've talked about selling this one, and if we use what you get for this one, and what I'll get from the beach house, we could find a bigger home." She held out the paper. "I've been looking at the listings by the Tatum Real Estate Agency, and there's one that sounds good to me.''

"Tatum Agency? Oh, that's Grover Tatum—he's a member of the Tyler Memorial Church, and the father of Don Tatum who goes to kindergarten with Eddie—you've heard Eddie talking about him.'' Alice nodded. "He was a difficult church member—always rather testy, but I guess he knows the real estate business.''

Mark looked through the property listings.

"Which house did you like?"

"This one," Alice said, pointing to a small ad, without a picture. "Antebellum home, twenty-five miles north of Richmond. An excellent location for a growing family."

"Antebellum? That's pre-Civil War vintage. Actually, I don't think we should consider buying a home now. If I'm called to another church, there might be a parsonage available."

"Most churches don't provide parsonages anymore, and we'll need a big house for our family. Will you go with me to see the property?"

Mark's face paled, and his hand tightened on Alice's shoulder. "My pride is still bothering me, but I won't object if you want to buy another house. You haven't made any decisions yet that haven't been good for the Tanner family."

"It has to be a joint decision. If we buy it now, perhaps it will be ready by the time we get married. I don't know how much renovation it will require."

"I'll telephone Tatum and make arrangements to see the property, and I'll take off one afternoon next week to go with you to look it over." He frowned and shook his head, "But I'm so busy trying to get my work finished at the bank, if we should decide to buy, I couldn't help you with other details."

"I'll soon be sharing your life, Mark, which means work and decisions, too—I can take care of the renovation details. Besides, I may not even like this house, but I would like to take a look at it."

Chapter Ten

A week later as they drove out of Richmond on I-95 to keep an appointment with Grover Tatum, Alice said, "One of the things I learned from John was that in buying a piece of property, the buyer shouldn't seem overly eager. So act disinterested when he shows us what he has."

"Whatever you say," he said, a wide smile on his face. Alice knew he was humoring her, seeing a new side to her personality, and finding it amusing.

They left the interstate on the Carmel Church exit and met Mr. Tatum at a nearby service area. Mark introduced Alice to Tatum as "my fiancée," the first time he'd done so, and Alice gave him a "thumbs-up."

Tatum had a toothy grin, and he shook hands with both of them. "So that's why you're looking for another house—gonna start a bigger family." Laughing loudly, Tatum continued, "Well, the old Ferguson property should be big enough to suit you, but it's mighty expensive for a preacher who's down on his luck to buy and maintain. It might be best if I show you some of the other listings I have in this area.''

"Let's take a look at the Ferguson house, anyway,'' Alice said. "I find old houses interesting.'' Tatum sighed, as if he knew he were wasting time showing them that piece of real estate.

A short drive brought them to property bordered by a stone fence along a stretch of rural highway. The agent stopped before a padlocked iron gate, bearing two No Trespassing signs. He unlocked the gate and left it ajar as he continued along a narrow lane bordered by ancient, gnarled oak trees. The driveway was a half-mile long, and it opened out to a wide expanse of unkempt lawn, surrounding a three-story brown brick antebellum home with massive brick chimneys at each end. To one side was a two-story wing that appeared to have been added sometime after the original house was built. A narrow portico supported by four round columns protected the white paneled door accessed by stone fan steps.

Tatum brought the car to a sudden stop, and said humorously, "There! That oughta be big enough for you.''

Alice's eyes brightened, and she winked at Mark.

"What do you think of it?'' Tatum said.

"We need a lot of room, but surely not that much,'' Mark said, and Alice knew he wasn't putting on an act. He didn't see anything enticing about the Ferguson estate.

Alice looked around. "It's rather run-down. How long has it been vacant?''

"The property has been in the Ferguson family for over two hundred years, and the last Ferguson died over a year ago. She was in her nineties then, and you're right, the house is run-down, as are the grounds. I'll be frank with you—there isn't much market for a place like this, because it isn't easy to find a buyer interested in this kind of house, who would have the money to buy and maintain it.''

As Tatum continued, Alice envisioned what a majestic home this must have been in its heyday, and her mind whirled with the possibilities of renovation.

''None of the heirs are interested in the place, and they're willing to sell for a good price, but it will take more to make the house livable than to buy it.'' Tatum surveyed the old brick dwelling. ''It's an interesting home. I'd like to see someone buy it and turn it into the showplace it was at one time.''

Alice winked at Mark again and gave his arm a little pinch, but his eyes met hers without comprehension.

''How much land goes with the house?'' he asked.

''Fifty acres.''

As they stepped out of the car, Alice noted a stone above the front door with the date, 1834. Considering the destruction by marauders during the Civil War, she marveled that this house remained intact, although she did see a few holes in the brick, that could have been caused by artillery.

Mark stepped on the wide fan steps, and one of the stones tilted. ''Careful,'' he said, taking Alice's arm.

The interior of the house was clammy and cool, and it smelled musty, but sunlight streaked through the dirty windows and added a hint of warmth. They stepped into a broad entrance hall, and along one side of the hall was a wide, paneled stairway that led to a landing on the second floor. Alice imagined a large grandfather clock on the second-floor landing and Kristin coming down the stairs in a voluminous wedding gown. The first and second floors of the central house each had four large rooms with ten-foot ceilings, containing some very fine dusty and cobwebby furniture.

"The furnishings are included in the price of the house," Tatum said.

When they would have gone to the third floor, he discouraged them. "I wouldn't go up there," he said. "Those steps are unstable."

"But how do you know about the structure of the house if you haven't seen that upper floor?" Mark asked.

"Oh, I've looked it over," Tatum said, "and if we get an interested buyer, I'll have a contractor repair the steps, but the heirs don't want to spend any money on the place until they have to."

When they entered the two-story wing, the agent said, "The last ten years or so, Miss Ferguson lived out here and seldom went into the main part of the house. She converted this wing into a little apartment."

The living area and a small kitchen were still furnished as it must have been in Miss Ferguson's day. The only bathroom in the house was located in the wing.

"Strange the heirs don't want any of these belongings," Alice said.

"Miss Ferguson's niece, the beneficiary in her will, is in her eighties, and as I understand, her family is financially well-off. There's nothing here that they need or want. Let's take a look in the backyard. The gardens were beautiful at one time.''

A ramshackle picket fence enclosed a large garden area, filled with weeds and untended flowers. Honeysuckle vines covered a few untrimmed boxwood. Dried hollyhock stalks rustled noisily in the light breeze. Alice shook her head at the neglect.

Beyond the garden were a barn and two smaller structures all made of hewn logs. The barn would provide a good place to stable horses for the children, and they'd have plenty of acreage for riding. Beyond the outbuildings, the landscape stretched upward toward low foothills. The place definitely had possibilities in Alice's opinion, but she had no idea what Mark thought of it.

''Thank you for showing us the place,'' Alice said, as they took leave of Tatum at the service station where'd they met him, ''but it is rather large, and we'll have to think about it. It must have been a beautiful home at one time.''

''We'll be in touch,'' Mark said.

They drove in silence a few miles, for Alice's mind was whirling, wondering whether it was a good idea to buy the property. ''You want it, don't you?'' Mark said at last. *So he could read her mind better than she thought he did!*

''It has terrific possibilities—plenty of room, an outdoor atmosphere for the children, a retreat for you at the end of a long day, and plenty of room for entertaining. If you accept another pastorate, you'll need to host many church functions. What did *you* think of it?''

''The place frightened me when I considered all the work needed to make it livable. I can't find time to take care of the property in Richmond, and when I thought of fifty acres to mow, I wanted to bolt. I'll admit the house did appeal to me for I've always liked old homes. It's out of the question anyway—it will cost too much money."

"But, Mark, we can hire someone to mow the lawn. We'll have enough money for extras. When you marry me, you're marrying my money. You'll be taking me 'for better or worse,' so you get the better along with the worst."

He grinned at her, reached out a hand and pulled her closer to him. "All, I've had so far is 'better,' I haven't discovered the 'worse,' yet."

"You will," she assured him, tugging on his ear-lobe and leaning over to kiss his hand resting on the steering wheel.

A serious expression crossed his face. "I can't get your money off my mind. I think about it all the time. The Bible speaks so forcefully on the danger of riches. 'Do not store up for yourselves treasures on earth...but store up for yourselves treasures in heaven...for where your treasure is, there your heart will be also.' I don't know how I can handle having all the money I want at my disposal. I'm yearning to be restored to a right relationship with God, and your money is a detriment. How can a rich pastor set a good example for his parishioners?"

"Mark, I told you—we'll give the money away."

"But I'm not sure that's right, either. Since you're so generous with the money, perhaps God is giving us an opportunity to use Larkin's money for His glory. It's a tough decision."

"I personally think we can do as much good with the money as various charities would. But I repeat, rather than have this money come between us, or in any way stand between you and your relationship to God, we're better off without it.''

Alice leaned her head on Mark's shoulder, and he dropped a quick kiss on her hair. ''Why should we be discussing money? This is the longest I've ever had you to myself. Let's talk about how much I love you.''

But Alice couldn't stop thinking about the Ferguson property, and finally Mark said, ''You know a minister's life is transient. If I'm called to a church in the Richmond area, it might be for a few years only, and I hate to see you get attached to the house and have to move off and leave it.''

''Mark, when I marry you, I'll marry your profession. If God calls you to be a missionary in the far reaches of the world, I'm going with you, and I'll instill that thought in the children's minds. If we put that house in the condition I'd like to, we'd be able to sell it at a profit. I'm sure it's a good investment. I don't want to do anything foolish, but I believe with the sale of the beach house and the home in Richmond, we'd have enough money to buy that property and restore it to its original splendor and not have to use any capital at all.''

''Sweetheart, I don't have any objections. You have more business experience than I do, so go ahead and check out your options. I'm just sorry I won't have time to help you.''

''We'll hire a contractor to do the work, for I wouldn't have time either. I'll be at home taking care of Gran and the children. But will you go with me to Alexandria on Saturday to talk to my accountant and let him check out the Ferguson land? John assured me that I could depend on any advice Mr. Haycraft gave me. I also want you to see my home."

"About this home in Alexandria—I suppose it's a mansion." His tone was light, and Alice knew he was slowly coming to terms with her money.

"It's not as big as the one we saw today," she said, "but it does have three floors, and when we add them to the furniture in your Richmond house, it has enough Larkin family heirlooms to furnish the Ferguson place."

"Will you sell the house in Alexandria?"

"No. Transitory government officials, many in the diplomatic service, like to rent houses close to D.C., and I can keep it rented all the time. It'll provide an extra income for us. After John died, I considered moving into an apartment and renting the house, because it was much too large for my needs, but I didn't know what to do with the furniture, so I stayed where I was."

Mark ruffled her hair, and his eyes were merry. "I always wondered what it would be like to be rich as Croesus, and I suppose I'll find out."

"Not unless you marry someone with a lot more assets than I have."

"Well, my dear, I have no intention of marrying anyone else. You're stuck with me."

"I believe I can handle that."

A week later Mr. Haycraft telephoned that he and a contractor had checked out the Ferguson property and considered it a well-built and stable house. It was their opinion that the property would be a good investment.

"Can you and Mark arrange to meet the contractor

and me at the Ferguson home tomorrow? I've gotten a good deal on the estate, but you should discuss anticipated renovations with the contractor and learn how much it will cost before you agree to buy. We have a ten-day option to close the deal.''

''Since it's Saturday, I think we can be there. My aunt and uncle are visiting in Richmond, and I'm sure they'll stay with the kids and Gran. Mark and I need to agree on what we want before we talk to the contractor, so we'll try to consolidate our ideas. Why don't we go a couple of hours before you do, so we can look around? We can get a key from Mr. Tatum, I suppose?''

''Yes, if he'll let you have it.'' Haycraft chuckled. ''He certainly is bemused that a preacher can afford the Ferguson property. I think if he'd known for sure that you were the purchasers, he might not have lowered the price when I approached him, but he didn't want to lose a sale. He seems to believe that all preachers should live just above the poverty level.''

''He knows that Mark has been in a financial bind for a couple of years, and he doesn't know anything about my money.''

''Is Mark as taken with the property as you are?''

''As long as Mark can provide a decent shelter for his family, he's not concerned much about where it is. And right now, he's busy finishing up some projects he initiated at the bank. He's hoping for a call to a church soon, and he wants to be free to resign his job when that call comes. He has no objections, and if I want to tackle the renovation of the house, he'll leave the matter up to me, but he's supportive.''

''I think you've made a good choice in a husband,

Alice, but I wonder if Mark has any idea how fortunate *he* is."

"I know how fortunate *I* am, and that's the only thing that matters to me."

Haycraft laughed. "Unless you hear differently within the next hour, we'll meet you at the Ferguson property, eleven o'clock, Saturday morning."

Alice went by the real estate office to pick up the key on Friday afternoon, and perhaps it was Mr. Haycraft's comments, but she, too, detected a difference in the Realtor's attitude.

While he fished in his desk drawer and pulled out the key to the Ferguson property, he said, "That house is going to take a lot of money to fix up."

"Probably so, but we'll find that out tomorrow."

"Seems funny for a preacher to have that much money."

"Of course, Mark hasn't been preaching for two years now, and he's had a good salary at the bank."

"Hear he's thinking about going back to preaching."

"He's trusting the leadership of the Spirit in that matter." Changing the subject, Alice said, "Eddie has mentioned that your son, Don, is taking riding lessons, and we want to get Eddie and Kristin enrolled at a stable. Do you recommend the instructors where your son goes?"

"Yes, I do," Tatum said grudgingly. "Don is an insecure child, and riding the pony has given him more confidence in what he can do."

"That's one reason we want to buy this home in the country—so we can have a place for the children to keep ponies."

* * *

Alice knew that the old house would be cold and damp, so she searched in the boxes she hadn't unpacked for a long insulated coat, and she found a heavy jacket in the closet that she'd brought along for Mark. When they entered the hallway, Alice didn't sense the welcome that she had the first day they'd come here, when the sun was shining and penetrating the cold interior. She shivered, and Mark put his arms around her.

"Be sure and put a furnace on your list," he said with a grin, as he pointed to the clipboard she carried.

"And some insulation for the walls," she agreed.

Each carrying a large flashlight, they made a survey of the two main floors. Alice opened the door to the third floor and flashed her light on the stairs. "I can't see a thing wrong with those stairs," she said. "I believe Mr. Tatum didn't want to take the time to show us the whole house."

"Remember, he thought he was dealing with a poor preacher. He couldn't see a pending sale."

Mark tried his weight on the bottom step. "Seems all right to me. I'll go up first just to be sure."

The steps did creak, and dust stirred around Mark's feet, but he reached the third floor without mishap, and Alice followed him. There was one long room that stretched the length of the house, and it was cluttered with boxes, trunks, and discarded furniture. Alice marveled at the breathtaking view from the dormer windows of the river valley to the west.

"We won't have to renovate this floor before we move in, but we can eventually make this area into two rooms and a bath. In a few years, Eddie may want to have his room on this floor. What do you think?"

"When I was a teenage boy, I'd have liked such a room." Mark was checking the structure of the house by looking at the exposed beams. "It seems that this house is structurally sound. I don't see any indication that the roof has ever leaked, nor any termite damage. I'll enjoy living here, and I don't have any objection to buying it, but I won't be of much help to you in the renovation. I don't even have any good ideas."

"Right now, I want you to make commitment to God's will your first priority. I'll take care of the family, the household and the renovation."

"I'll support anything you want to do, and I'll give any suggestions I'm capable of making."

Back on the first floor, they decided that they'd retain Miss Ferguson's apartment as a kitchen, a family dining area, and television room. The four large downstairs rooms would be turned into a bedroom for Gran, a company dining room, living room and an office for Mark. The rooms on the second floor would provide a guest room, and rooms for Kristin, Eddie, and the two of them.

"We'd better have two bathrooms upstairs," Mark said. "Kristin is getting to the primping stage, and I don't want to fight her for the bathroom all the time."

"We can make a private bathroom from our room, and one at the end of the corridor. We'll put a bathroom downstairs for Gran, and keep the small lavatory near the kitchen."

"Alice, you cannot take care of all of this property alone."

"I don't intend to. The housekeeper I have in Alexandria has agreed to come here, and she'll do all the cleaning. Her husband will be the outside caretaker, and all I'll have to do is cook, look after the family, and keep my husband happy.''

He lifted his eyebrows and kissed her. ''And that will take a lot of time. But where is the housekeeper going to live?''

''Let's check outdoors. There's a two-story log building that looks as if it might have been a garage. That could be made into a delightful home.''

When they went through the garden on their way to the building, Alice paused to say, ''We'll have this fence repaired, too. Can't you envision this full of flowers and shrubbery? We'll have a gazebo built in one end.''

''Right now, I can't envision anything but a cold, winter morning, with the wind blowing and my nose getting cold.''

''And I thought you were a romantic!''

''Oh, I can be romantic enough, but not when my feet and hands are cold. Let's check out this building and then go find a cozy restaurant with some hot food.'' He smiled at her. ''I have no doubt that you'll make this into the coziest home in Virginia, where all of us will be content.''

Alice rubbed her hand across his cold face and kissed his cheek.

The log house was in good repair, and both of them agreed that it could be made into a lovely home. The downstairs could be living and kitchen quarters, and the upper floor reached by an open stairway would make a cozy bedroom and a bathroom.

''Pretty small for a residence, isn't it?'' Mark asked.

"The housekeeper will be working in our house most of the day, and she won't want a large home to care for. They wouldn't have much company, for they don't have any children, but if any of their extended family comes to visit, they can always use the guest room in the big house. We'll build to suit their needs."

Mark laughed at her. "I've never seen anyone more generous with money than you. I believe you like playing Santa Claus."

"It does give me a satisfying feeling," Alice admitted.

"What better way to fulfill the command of the Scripture, 'Whoever sows sparingly will also reap sparingly, and whoever sows generously will also reap generously...for God loves a cheerful giver'? I've been given money that John and his ancestors accumulated—I really don't feel as if it belongs to me, only that I'm the steward. John was very generous with those who worked for him or wherever he saw a need. I learned the example from him, not from my parents."

Mark's eyes were glowing and he pulled Alice close. "I know a few verses of Scripture, too, and one that I believe applies to you was when Jesus said, 'Give and it shall be given to you.' I don't know what God has in mind for you, Alice, but it's bound to be a great life. He'll reward you for your generosity."

"The day God gives you to me, I'll have everything. You and your children are all I want."

"Don't you want a child of your own?"

"Very much so, but I'm in my midthirties, and it may not be a good idea."

Mark bent his lips to hers, and both of them forgot the cold, blustery winter weather buffeting them. They didn't mind at all the half-hour wait for the contractor and Mr. Haycraft. Now that they'd definitely agreed to be married, the two of them had relaxed the strict hands-off policy that they'd stuck to so rigidly during her first months in the house. Even yet, they held their emotions in check, but they found no reason to refrain from occasional hugs and kisses. Alice hadn't doubted that the emotional relationship between her and Mark would be fulfilling, but she hadn't expected the camaraderie they enjoyed. Not only were they sweethearts, they were also best friends.

The contractor agreed with most of their plans, and they took his suggestions about changes in the house to make it more livable and economical on utilities. The price he quoted for repairs was reasonable, according to Haycraft, and Alice and Mark relied on his advice.

"And how long will it take you to do this work?" Alice said.

"Six months, if I don't run into any trouble."

Alice groaned. "That seems like a long time."

"Now, Mrs. Larkin," he said, "you want this work done right, and it will take longer to renovate than if you had me build a new house. By the time we remove the old plaster, insulate the walls and ceilings, install new walls, sand the floors, and repair and refinish all of the woodwork, it takes time."

"And we shouldn't move in until it's completely finished," Mark said.

"You mentioned that you'd refurbish the third floor at a later time," Haycraft said. "May I suggest that you do that now? It won't delay you much longer, and if you do it later, think of all the dirt the workers will make carrying supplies up to that area.''

Alice threw up her hands. ''I didn't think of that— I was mostly interested in time. That's the reason John told me I could rely on you to set me straight.'' To the contractor, she said, ''Go ahead and finish that floor—make two rooms and a bathroom.''

''We can decide about fixtures and other ideas as we go along,'' the contractor said.

''I'm sorry that I won't be of much help to you or Alice,'' Mark apologized, ''but Alice has a better head for business than I do anyway.''

''She had a good teacher in John Larkin,'' Haycraft said.

Acting on the advice of Mr. Tatum, Alice and Mark took Eddie and Kristin to a riding stable a few miles from their home. Eddie was enthusiastic about the idea of learning to ride, but Kristin was reluctant.

''You don't have to participate in this, Kristin,'' Alice assured her as they drove to the stables. ''We're simply giving you the opportunity. Perhaps you'd like another activity, and that will be fine. You can make up your own mind about it.''

''Can I really have my own horse when we get moved?'' Eddie asked.

''It will have to be a pony for a few years, but if you learn to ride and take care of the pony, you can have one of your own,'' Mark said. ''The contractor will be renovating the barn into a riding stable as soon as he finishes with the house. You'll have plenty of space to ride on our property.''

''Will you have a horse, too, Daddy?''

"I will, according to Alice," Mark said, with a tender smile in Alice's direction. "She thinks riding will be a good family activity, but I haven't ridden a horse for years."

"Neither have I," Alice said, "so all of us can learn together. It will be relaxing pastime for you after the pressure of your job."

"Kristin is a sissy if she doesn't want to ride."

That comment convinced Kristin, that if the rest of the family had horses, she was determined to have one, too. She wasn't going to have her daddy doing something with Eddie that she couldn't do.

The lessons did go well, and Alice was impressed with the academy's instructors. Noting the children's rapid progress, she thought the two-hour lessons each Saturday morning were well worth the time and money they spent. The children rode Shetland ponies, and Alice and Mark were mounted on American quarter horses.

And then the murmurings started!

Friends whom Alice had made at Tyler Memorial started avoiding her, many dropping their gazes when she entered the church with Mark and his family. After this went on for a few weeks, she went to see Betty.

"What's going on, Betty?"

Betty didn't pretend that she didn't know what Alice meant.

"I wondered how long it would be before you found out. I should have told you, but I've been so angry I couldn't talk about it."

"Talk about what?" Alice demanded.

"Ethel Pennington! She's spreading rumors that

you and Mark are having an affair 'right under the same roof with his kids,' to quote her exact words, and when she accused him of it, Mark ordered her out of the house.''

Alice slumped down in a chair. ''I knew this would happen. I should have left months ago. I'll go back to Alexandria until we're married.''

''And send Eddie into a decline that might kill him?''

''I've only stayed for Eddie's sake, but he's stronger now. He'll be all right.''

''Don't be hasty in that decision,'' Betty advised. ''Perhaps this will blow over as most gossip does.''

Chapter Eleven

A few nights later when Mark came home, after he'd checked the day's mail that Alice always placed on the hall table, he came immediately to the kitchen with a letter in his hand. His face was gray as ashes.

"What's wrong, Mark?" Alice said and went to his side.

He dropped down in a kitchen chair and handed her the letter.

"It's a letter from the ordination committee of our state convention, asking me to appear before them to answer charges of gross immorality. If they find the charges to be true, they'll withdraw my ordination."

"What does that mean?"

"It means I would never get another position of any kind in our denomination. I've wondered why I haven't been approached by any churches after I submitted my name as a pastoral candidate. This must be the reason."

"This accusation has apparently originated from rumors that Ethel spread about our relationship."

"The pastor of Tyler Memorial mentioned the rumors to me, but I hoped you wouldn't hear anything." He put an arm around Alice's waist and pulled her close to him.

"There's only one thing to do—I'll go back to Alexandria and stay until we can be married, Mark, but not until you've dealt with this." She lifted the letter and read it. "That meeting is next week. I won't leave until after that, for I'm going to the meeting with you. My reputation, as well as yours, is at stake. I see the meeting will be held at the local church."

"Yes, but the board members are from all over the state." Mark laid his head against Alice, and she bent over and kissed his forehead. "I want you to go with me, but I wouldn't have asked." He shook his head, "I don't see how Ethel's suspicions could have influenced the state ordination board, but one never knows. Be in prayer about the situation. If there's any doubt about our relationship, we have to put it to rest now, or it will follow us wherever we go."

"'If our hearts do not condemn us, we have confidence before God and receive from him anything we ask, because we obey his commands and do what pleases Him,'" Alice reminded him.

"That's true. The months you've been in this house, it hasn't been easy to keep my distance, but I was as determined as you that our relations would be open and aboveboard."

Alice's nerves had never been more jittery than when she walked into the conference room the next week. The last thing in the world she wanted was to cause shock waves for Mark's ministry. They arrived at the church a few minutes before the hour of the appointment, and she waited in the entrance hall until Mark got permission from the board for her to sit in on the meeting. When a man came and motioned for her to enter, Alice eased down in a chair by the door, miserable and self-conscious, as every eye in the room turned toward her. She might as well have had a scarlet letter emblazoned on her blouse!

Mark patted a vacant chair beside him. "You come and sit here, please, Alice."

The presiding board member was Reverend Astor, the man she'd met at church camp in the summer. Since he was a good friend of Mark's, she hoped that he could sway the deliberations in Mark's favor.

After clearing his throat a few times, Reverend Astor said, "This is a painful meeting for me, Mark, and I know it must be for you. However, charges have been brought before this board on the basis of circulating rumors, and while most of the board members feel the charges are unjustified, you should have a chance to defend yourself."

"What are the charges?"

"That you and Mrs. Larkin are involved in an illicit relationship, and that she's bought your affections with a huge outlay of money. In addition to that, we've had a complaint about your ethics in a business deal."

Alice sensed Mark's rising anger, and she rather forcefully took hold of his arm and kicked his foot slightly.

"Mrs. Pennington, who's your neighbor and a member of this church, charges that Mrs. Larkin has been living in your home for several months."

"There isn't any secret about that. Alice came in

May as housekeeper and a nanny for my two children."

"But it seems there's more to your relationship than that," Astor said.

"We fell in love immediately," Mark admitted, "but we haven't done anything to bring reproach on either of us. We haven't been alone in the house— my two kids and Gran Watson are there all the time. I sleep upstairs with the rest of the family, Alice sleeps in a downstairs room, a long way from mine. You'll have to take our word for it, for I won't have you questioning my children or Gran."

"I do believe you, Brother Tanner," Reverend Astor said.

"To be honest, it isn't that we haven't wanted more than that, but our relationships have been honest. We plan to marry, but it isn't because we *have* to get married."

"In her letter, Mrs. Pennington states that you ordered her out of your house when she accused you of an affair," Astor continued.

"I asked her to leave the house, and stay away, because she was meddling in the discipline of my children. Her accusations against Alice and me aren't true."

Alice spoke for the first time. "Since modesty will keep Mark from telling you this, I will. In case you hadn't noticed, he's a very attractive man, and long before Mark's first wife died, Ethel pursued him rather ruthlessly. She was in and out of the house, ingratiating herself with Gran and the children. Those of you who live in Richmond know that. When she learned that Mark and I planned to marry, she encouraged Kristin and Gran to fight our plans. That's when Mark refused to have her come to the house or to contact his children. In other words, I accomplished in a few months what she'd set out to do, and she's jealous.''

Several of the board members laughed, and the tension in the room lightened.

''There's little we can do about her accusations, except go on living as we have, knowing that we haven't done anything to be ashamed of,'' Mark said. ''And if you find us innocent of this charge, it will indicate that you consider our relationship is, and has always been, circumspect.''

Alice sensed that the board was behind them, and that they were somewhat ashamed that they'd even called this meeting.

''I believe you've answered our questions about the immorality accusation, now we need to deal with the ethics charge.''

''You didn't say who brought that charge,'' Mark said, and Alice wondered if the accuser was someone Mark had dealt with at the bank.

''The agent who recently handled a real estate purchase for you,'' Astor said.

''Mr. Tatum?'' Alice said in an incredulous tone. Astor nodded.

''Then we need to hear directly from Mr. Tatum,'' Mark said. ''He lives nearby— Could he be asked to appear before this board?''

The pastor of the Tyler Memorial Church was one of the board members and he stood. ''Mr. Tatum is in the church now at a trustee's meeting—we could ask him to come in for a few minutes.''

''Please do,'' Mark said, and his face was white, his features tense.

While Mr. Tatum was being summoned, the pastor continued, "I want to apologize to Brother Tanner, as well as Mrs. Larkin, for this meeting tonight. I realize when the board was presented with these charges, you had no choice except to investigate. However, the majority of the members here in the local church are indignant and embarrassed by these events. Mark Tanner was an effective pastor of this church for several years, and we have in the building now a delegation of more than one hundred people, led by Betty St. Claire, who've come as character witnesses for Mark and Mrs. Larkin."

"Thank you, Pastor," Reverend Astor said. "I doubt they'll be needed, but their support is appreciated."

Grover Tatum's face paled, and he gasped slightly, when he entered the room and saw Mark and Alice.

"Mr. Tatum," Mark said as pleasantly as if he were discussing the weather, "we've learned that you've accused us of unethical dealings when we purchased the Ferguson property. We'd appreciate it if you'd tell us why you think that."

The Realtor's face turned a mottled red and white, and his eyes darted from one person to another, although he carefully avoided looking at Mark and Alice. He swallowed convulsively a few times, and then he blurted out belligerently, "They cost me a tidy sum in closing fees."

"Could you explain?" Reverend Astor asked.

"Because he was a minister, I dropped the price several thousand dollars."

"Right, when you quoted us a price on the property, you said the owners would take quite a bit less to make a sale." Mark said.

"It's not right for a preacher to take advantage of me. I thought you were hard up. If you have enough money to buy that place and fix it up, you should have purchased at the asking price instead of driving a hard bargain with me. Preachers are supposed to be ethical."

Mark smiled. "And the same rule doesn't apply to Realtors, I suppose?"

"Mr. Tatum," Alice asked, "how much money did you lose because we took you at your word and asked for the lowest possible price?" She reached in her purse, took out her checkbook and waited for his reply.

"At least two hundred dollars."

Alice made out a check in that amount. "Then we'll pay you the additional fee rather than to have our honesty questioned." She gave the check to the man on her right. "Will you pass this check to Mr. Tatum?"

When he got the check in his hand, Tatum turned it over and over, as if he didn't know what to do with it, and finally blurted out, "It doesn't seem right somehow, for a preacher to have so much money. I thought preachers were servants of the Lord and of people."

It took a lot to make Alice angry, but she couldn't stand much more of this, and she knew that Mark was near the breaking point. She again laid a cautionary hand on Mark's arm—the wrong words could ruin his future.

Quietly, he said, "*I* don't have any money, Mr. Tatum. If Alice wants to say anything, that's up to her."

Reverend Astor rose. "I feel this conversation has

gone far enough. In the first place, Brother Tanner isn't guilty of anything more than buying a piece of property at a reasonable price, and from what I've heard, he still paid more for the Ferguson place than it's worth. Secondly, I believe that Mr. Tatum has an antiquated idea about the finances of our pastors. Today, we provide an adequate salary for those in the ministry so their families won't have a substandard living.''

Several ''amens'' indicated general agreement to this statement.

''I'm sorry,'' Astor continued, ''that I've had the misfortune to preside over a meeting that has cast reflections on the reputation of one of the best pastors in our convention. I'll entertain a motion that these charges be dropped and never brought up again.''

A quick motion and second were received, but before the vote was taken, Alice said, ''May I speak frankly? I don't consider my financial status any of your business when my money came from a legitimate source, but when my assets might reflect upon Mark's position as a minister, I'm going to explain.''

Alice hesitated, wondering how much to say, praying for the right attitude to overcome her annoyance.

''I inherited a rather large sum of money from my late husband, and that's where most of the money came from to buy the property in question. But we're not expecting that outlay of money to benefit us only. When I envisioned renovating the Ferguson property, it wasn't exclusively for our use, but I planned to have a comfortable setting for visiting evangelists, missionaries, and for church meetings when Mark takes another pastorate. I hosted many social gatherings for my husband, and I enjoy entertaining.''

A woman, halfway down the table from Alice, who hadn't said a word, timidly raised her hand. The chairman asked her to speak.

"I don't want to offend Mrs. Larkin because I've never credited any of the stories we've heard, but I want to pose a question that I think others may ask someday. If you're so affluent, why did you go to work as a nanny and housekeeper?"

"I went to the Tanners upon the request of my friend, Betty St. Claire, who's a member of this church. I'd been confined for several years taking care of my invalid husband, and after he died, my life was rather aimless. I needed something to do and when I considered going back to kindergarten teaching, Betty, who runs a nanny agency, asked me to go to the Tanners. Mark and his two children were hurting over the death of their wife and mother, and Betty thought the situation would be beneficial to all of us. I've always loved children, and I was willing to go. It was a long time before Mark knew I had any money."

Alice could feel the tears building, and with a little sob, she said, "When I accepted the job, I believed that God had called me to be of service to the Tanners. I didn't intend to love Mark and his children, but I do, and I believe that is God's will, too."

Most of the people at the table wouldn't meet Alice's eyes, but the woman who'd posed the question smiled and said, "I believe that, too. God bless you, my dear."

The crisis passed, but several days later when they heard that the church board had asked the Tatums and Ethel to withdraw their membership from the

Tyler Memorial Church, Alice and Mark were stunned.

"How could we have handled the situation differently?" Mark asked.

"I don't know. Perhaps I made a mistake to come to your home, but in my heart, I can't believe that."

"Neither do I," Mark agreed, "but I'm going to pray that God will give us the opportunity to make amends."

Alice and the children often encountered Mrs. Tatum and her son, Don, at the riding stables, but they ignored the Tanner children. Alice was especially disturbed that the Tatum boy wouldn't speak to Eddie, who had become a friendly, outgoing child.

Whenever his schedule permitted, Mark went with them to the stables on Saturday mornings, and the four of them enjoyed the two hours they spent together learning proper riding skills and techniques and how to care for their mounts. When it became apparent that the two children were interested in riding, and that it wasn't a passing whim, Mark and Alice decided to buy two ponies and a couple of horses and board them at the stables until they could move them to their new home.

But the day when they needed him the most, Mark had a meeting at the bank and couldn't go riding with them. It was a balmy morning, and the sun was shining brightly. Alice and the kids waited until Don Tatum and his mother started around the paddock before they mounted. Because of the anger the Tatums held toward her and Mark, Alice wouldn't crowd them on their ride.

They were having a pleasant ride until Eddie

shouted, "Look at those dogs running across the field."

Three dogs scampered across the field, and a rabbit bounded a few feet in front of them, heading toward the riding ring. The dogs, baying loudly, chased the rabbit toward the Tatums, and all four of them ran underneath Don's pony. The frightened animal whinnied in fear, and kicked its rear legs at the dogs.

Mrs. Tatum screeched, "Help!" which only frightened the terrified animal more. The pony started to run, and screaming, Don tried to dismount, but he slipped from the saddle, and one foot caught in the stirrup as the animal bolted.

Alice kicked her mount into action, thankful that she was riding Mark's faster horse today. She soon overtook Don and the pony. Jumping from the saddle, she grabbed the boy and jerked his leg loose from the stirrup. She shielded Don with her body as they fell to the ground, but she struck her head on a metal post. Except for his fear, Don was unharmed and he ran to his mother; but as Alice fell, the pony lashed out with its hooves, striking her arm. She saw Eddie and Kristin racing toward her before she blacked out.

Mark was leaving his office when the phone rang. Recognizing the voice of the manager at the stables, his first thought was that one of the children had been hurt. He wasn't prepared for the man's message.

"Mrs. Larkin has had an accident, and I'm afraid she's seriously injured." He briefly outlined what had happened. "I've already contacted 911, and the ambulance is on the way. It's probably better if you meet them at the hospital. Do you want me to take your kids home?''

''No, bring them to the hospital—they'll want to be with us.''

Mark paused to telephone Gran and let her know what had happened, then he ran to his station wagon, arriving at the hospital just as the ambulance backed into the emergency room entrance. He parked hurriedly, and was by the ambulance door when the attendants removed Alice.

''Oh, Alice,'' Mark whispered when he saw her. Her face was chalky, except for a large bruise on her forehead, and even though she was unconscious, she groaned in pain when they moved the cot from the ambulance.

Feeling someone tugging on his hand, Mark turned to find Kristin and Eddie beside him.

''Oh, Daddy, it was terrible,'' Kristin said, ''but she was so brave. It was just like something out of the movies—Don Tatum wasn't hurt at all.''

''Is Alice hurt bad?'' Eddie asked, his lips quivering.

Mark knelt and put his arms around them. ''I don't know, but will you be good kids and sit here in the waiting room? I'll see what I can find out.''

Since Mark was well-known at the hospital, the staff made no objection when he entered the examining room to wait with bated breath for the diagnosis.

''Her left arm is broken, and it looks as if it's a clean break,'' the doctor said, ''but that's the least of her problems. I don't like this knot on her head, which is probably a concussion. She'll probably regain consciousness in a few hours, but we'll have to admit her for observation. She also has several cracked ribs, which will pain her more than the broken bone.''

Mark nodded. ''Arrange for a private room—my children and I will want to stay with her. We won't leave until I know how badly she's hurt.''

Alice was taken to X-ray, and her arm set before she was assigned to a room.

Betty St. Claire and many other friends of Alice and Mark soon arrived, but Mark met them in the corridor for he didn't want Alice to be disturbed. They'd come to offer help with the children, to take care of Gran, or to do anything else that was needful.

Even Grover Tatum and his wife came—ashamed and remorseful—to find out the extent of Alice's injuries. With a break in his voice, Tatum said, ''My wife told me how she saved our boy's life. If it hadn't been for her, our son might be here instead of her.''

Mark accepted all offers of help and sympathy with a smile and thank-you, and he asked for their prayers. When the well-wishers left, Mark telephoned the desk and asked them to post a No Visitors, sign on the door. He knelt between Kristin and Eddie who looked small and defenseless as they huddled in their chairs.

''It's time we prayed for Alice,'' he said. Reaching out a hand to both of them, he closed his eyes. ''God, we come to you on Alice's behalf. We pray for healing, and we believe that You will answer. We can't believe, God, that when you've given Alice to us that You'd take her away after such a short time. But whatever happens, we thank you for the time we've had her, and for the difference she's made in our lives. Amen.''

Kristin was sniffling, and Mark found a tissue for her. ''I'm sorry I've been mean to Alice, Daddy. You know I love her, don't you?''

He hugged his daughter. ''Of course, I know you love her, and Alice knows it, too.''

Mark stood beside the bed and held the hand that wasn't connected to an IV, and he thought she might have returned the slight pressure of his clasp. Alice's color was more natural now, but the left side of her face was turning black. Mark suddenly remembered his prayer asking for an opportunity to reach the Tatums, but he hadn't expected this. Sometimes prayers could be risky.

By late afternoon, there was no change, but Mark knew the children needed a break, so he took them to the cafeteria. He debated whether to send them home, but when he broached the subject, they raised such a ruckus that he didn't insist.

Besides, he knew that Alice would want to see them when she wakened.

The results of the X-rays were positive, and her vital signs were good, so the doctors predicted that Alice would make a complete recovery. They expected her to awaken before many hours.

The nurses brought blankets, and he made the kids as comfortable as possible in the chairs. Mark sat beside the bed, watching the even flow of her breathing, smiling as he reviewed the events that had brought them together. He remembered the first day he'd seen her and the immediate attraction between them. He thought of the first time he'd kissed her, about his proposal at the beach and her quick acceptance. He remembered the many things she'd done to make him feel special...wanted...*loved.*

He considered how willing she was to forgive those who had wronged her—of how she'd forgiven Kristin and Gran for their unjustified treatment. She didn't hold a grudge against Ethel, the Tatums, or her parents, who took her for granted.

It was well after midnight when Mark felt Alice's hand move slightly, and she opened her eyes.

"Mark?" she whispered.

"Right here, sweetheart."

"Kristin and Eddie?"

"Asleep in chairs on the other side of the room. Do you want me to wake them?"

She shook her head and groaned.

"How badly am I hurt?"

"There's a knot on your head the size of a baseball, a broken arm and some cracked ribs, but the doctor says you'll live," he added with a smile.

"I have a terrific headache."

"I'll ring for a nurse. Now that you're awake, they'll give you something for that."

"How's Don Tatum?"

"In good shape, thanks to you."

"I suppose what I did was stupid, but I acted without thinking."

"A good thing for Don that you did. The manager of the stables said he could easily have been killed if you hadn't gotten him off the pony."

When the nurse answered Mark's summons, she turned on the light and awakened Kristin and Eddie. They ran to the bed and Mark moved aside to let them take the place he'd occupied all night.

"Arm hurt, Alice?" Eddie asked anxiously, and

Alice was reminded of the time he'd been hit in the stomach with the softball.

"Not as much as my head and ribs," she said. She reached out her hand and both of them grabbed it.

"We prayed for you," Kristin said. "We're so proud of you, 'specially when you saved Don after his daddy has been so mean to you. And I'm awful sorry for the way I've acted the past few months. I want you to be our mother."

Mark and Alice exchanged amazed glances. They'd had no idea the children knew about the charges brought against Mark, for they'd carefully avoided mention of the trouble Mr. Tatum and Ethel had caused when the kids were around.

"Maybe you'll have your picture in the paper," Eddie said.

Alice started to shake her head, but remembered that wasn't a good idea. The shot the nurse had given her began to take effect, and she closed her eyes. The voices of Mark and the nurse sounded far away.

Alice was released from the hospital after two days, but she wouldn't be able to work for several weeks, and Mark inquired about some part-time help.

"That's a bit much, Mark," she said, "hiring help to take care of the hired help." She insisted on going to a nursing home until she was able to work again, but that request brought a resounding no from all the Tanners.

Although Alice spent much of her time in her bedroom, she did go into the family room after dinner on her second night at home. While Mark and Kristin were rinsing dishes, the doorbell rang, and when Mark answered, Ethel Pennington stood on the steps.

Mark was speechless for a few minutes, as he stared at Ethel. She spoke first.

"I've come to help out."

"Come in, Ethel," he said.

"I won't come in now—I wanted to find out what needs to be done."

Eddie and Kristin ran to Ethel, grabbed her hands and pulled her into the house. They were glad to see her, and rightfully so, for she'd been their friend during those difficult days when their mother was dying.

Mark exchanged glances with Alice, and she nodded.

"Sit down, Ethel," Alice invited.

Ethel perched on the edge of a chair, ill at ease.

"I'm going to play T-ball this summer," Eddie said.

"We've got some new ponies, too, but I don't know if I want to ride anymore after what happened to Don," Kristin said, and Eddie's eyes grew large in fright.

Alice and Mark had anticipated this reaction, and he said evenly, "Of course, we're going to continue riding. That was a rare accident, and not likely to happen again. You'll be perfectly safe after you've taken more lessons and know how to handle your mount."

"Buffy wouldn't have scared the pony," Eddie said.

Ethel's eyes darted to Alice. "Are you hurt very much?"

"Nothing that won't heal eventually, and I'm not in a great deal of pain if I don't move quickly. We do need some help, and it's good of you to offer."

"What can I do?"

"Mark is doing all right with breakfast and getting the children ready for school, but if you could come for a few hours in the afternoon to clean, do laundry and prepare the evening meal, it would be a big help."

Ethel stood up. "I'll be here at noon tomorrow and prepare some lunch for you."

Eddie took a book from the coffee table. "This is a book I brought from the school library. Why don't you read to me, Ethel?"

Ethel looked quickly at Mark. "You're welcome to stay," he said, and she sat down again and Eddie stood beside her chair while she read. Ethel stayed for an hour, and the awkwardness of her visit eased considerably. When she finally left, she paused by the door, and without looking at them, she said, "I'm sorry for what happened in the past. I hope you'll forgive me."

"You were forgiven a long time ago, Ethel," Mark said. "The past is gone—let's forget it."

While Mark supervised the children's showers and bundled them into bed, Alice carefully walked to her room. The least movement was agony to her bruised body, but she was determined she wouldn't add to Mark's workload, and she waited on herself as much as possible. She'd removed her robe and had eased into bed when Mark came to check on her.

He sat on the edge of the bed and took her hand. "That's certainly a strange turn of events."

"Yes, but one that brought a lot of peace to my mind and heart. I've always been uncomfortable about my attitude toward Ethel. I should ask *her* forgiveness."

"I know what you mean. It was despicable of me

to order her from our home, and I'm more than willing to let bygones be bygones. It will teach me humility to accept help from a woman I treated so badly.''

''I've always felt sorry for Ethel. I think she does love you, and loving you as much as I do, if you'd chosen Ethel instead of me, I might have been a poor loser, too.''

Mark bent over and kissed Alice softly, careful not to disturb her injuries. How he wished they'd gotten married before this happened! He wanted to lie beside her and comfort her with his presence, but he didn't have that right—yet.

During the next two weeks, Ethel was true to her word. And without the worry of the household, Alice healed rapidly. Ethel was always busy when she was in the house, and she didn't give Alice an opportunity to talk with her. But one afternoon when Ethel was in the kitchen preparing dinner, Alice eased out of bed and walked slowly into the room and put two cups of water in the microwave for quick heating.

''Why don't you take a break and join me for a cup of tea, Ethel? I'd like to talk to you. I believe you take sugar in your tea.''

Ethel didn't reply, but when Alice had the water boiling and had placed the cups on the table, Ethel sat down.

''I'm asking you to forgive me, Ethel. I should have been more understanding of your situation. You'd been good to Mark and his family, and I do appreciate it. We didn't treat you very well, and I'm sorry for that.''

Ethel's face flushed and her eyes filled with tears.

"I did love him," she said, "and I thought he'd turn to me when Clarice died. Of course, I know now, you're the one for him. You'll be a better mother than I could be, but it's hard to accept."

Alice reached across the table and put her hand over Ethel's tense fingers. "I can't apologize for wanting to marry Mark, for I love him very much, but I am sorry that you can't be happy, too."

"I'll get over it," Ethel said, swiping tears from her eyes. "It's not the first disappointment I've had. Being here in the house has made it easier, although I dreaded to come back."

"Can't we be friends? It would mean a great deal to the children, for you're one of the few ties they have to their mother. Besides, Mark and I don't like to be at odds with anyone."

"When are you going to get married?"

"I don't know. Mark wants to wait until he feels the definite leading of the Spirit for his future. When he's so unsettled—not knowing where he might be called to serve—we decided to wait. And, of course, Eddie and Kristin need to get used to the idea."

After a month, the doctor checked Alice and, with a light brace on her arm, he said she could resume her household duties with caution. Ethel discontinued her daily visits, but she went with the Tanners' standing invitation to visit them at any time, especially when they moved into their renovated home and had a spare bedroom.

Alice was still not up to her usual activities, and after she got the children off to school the day after her trip to the doctor, she sat in the family room to read her Bible and pray. The last two months had been so full of trauma and pain, both physical and mental, that she had trouble sorting out the good and the bad, but as she thought about it, she decided that the good outweighed the bad. She couldn't wish away the bad days when she considered the positive results of the charges against Mark and her near-tragic accident.

The appearance before the Ordination Committee, and the dropping of the charges against Mark, had improved his standing with the state organization, rather than having an adverse effect. Several churches had already contacted him with tentative proposals for ministry.

And her accident had brought some needed reconciliation with her family, too. Her parents, who'd been standoffish since she'd refused to finance a house for Nancy, had come to see her at the Tanner home, and after staying in Richmond a few days had gone home convinced that her decision to marry Mark was a good one. Since Alice had awakened in the hospital, Kristin's attitude had changed, and more than once, she apologized for her earlier treatment of Alice. Gran had been as attentive as her disability permitted during the days of Alice's recuperation.

Alice had only one worry—why did Mark still hesitate to marry her? She knew it had nothing to do with his love for Clarice. The children were no longer objecting, and Eddie asked almost every day when they were going to get married. Any question about an immoral relationship between them had been aired to the community and they'd been pronounced innocent. What made Mark reluctant to set a date? Was he still worried about the money she'd inherited?

But she learned the truth about Mark's hesitancy

when he breezed into the kitchen that evening. He'd telephoned that he had an appointment and would be later than usual. Alice was busy at the stove, and for the first time since her accident, he put his arms around her. She winced a little, saying, "My ribs are still tender, Mark. Be careful."

He dropped his arms and bent to kiss her. "Sorry, but I'm so happy to see you standing there that I had to touch you. And I have some outstanding news, too. I've just come from a meeting with the official board of Tyler Memorial Church. The pastor is resigning, and they want me to come back as their senior minister."

"Oh, Mark! Is that what you want to do?"

"Yes, it is, although I didn't know it. When I learned what they wanted, the most outstanding sense of peace and comfort entered my heart. I've been fearful that God no longer had a place for me in His service, especially after I was so wayward in trusting Him during the crises of my life. When I've had interviews with other church boards, I felt nothing— no enthusiasm, no interest in their propositions. Now I know why—God expected me to take up the cross I laid down at this local church two years ago."

"When will you start, Mark?"

"Their pastor doesn't leave for two months—that will give me ample time to tender my resignation at the bank. When can we get married?" he added eagerly.

So it was spiritual anxiety that had kept him from marriage!

"Let's sit down, Mark. I've been up more today than usual."

He held the chair for her as she sat at the table.

"The contractor telephoned today, and he says that the renovations have gone well, and we can move in a couple of months, which will be after the first of the year. But let's be married sooner than that—perhaps before Christmas.

"Sounds good to me."

"If I can get Aunt Margaret to come and look after Gran and the kids, I'll go to Alexandria and prepare to close that house as soon as my ribs heal. I need to choose the furniture that I'll leave there and what I'll bring to our new home. If Aunt Margaret will come, I won't feel rushed."

"Then, I assume that you have no objection to my return to the local church. I told the board that I wouldn't give an answer until I talked it over with you."

"That's sweet of you, Mark, but I'll be delighted to continue worshiping there. All of us have many friends at Tyler Memorial, and I especially appreciate the support they gave us during your hearing with the ordination board."

Chapter Twelve

The insistent ringing of the doorbell awakened Alice, and for a moment she was tempted to ignore it. She hadn't activated her telephone service for the few days she intended to be in Alexandria, and she couldn't imagine who would even know she was here.

She wasn't sleeping well, for the extra exertion of cleaning closets and tugging on furniture was arduous, making her realize she wasn't fully recovered from the accident. Her arm had hurt all night, and she'd counted the passage of time by listening to the grandfather clock in the lower hall tolling the hours. It had been past four o'clock when she'd gone to sleep. Noting that it was only seven o'clock, she rolled out of bed and slipped into a robe as she hurried downstairs. She looked through the peephole before she opened the door.

Betty!

"What's wrong?" she said breathlessly, as she admitted Betty St. Claire to the house.

"Eddie's sick."

Alice stumbled into the living room to the right of the hallway. She dropped heavily into an antique chair and motioned Betty to sit down.

"Is it his heart again?"

"The doctors don't think so, but the malady is hard to diagnose. It's a bacterial infection of some kind. He got sick at school the day after you left. Whatever it is, it's really sapped his strength."

"How bad is he?"

"Bad enough that Mark wanted me to come and get you. He didn't think he should leave."

"Dr. Zane warned us that Eddie would be more susceptible to sickness than other children. His condition must be serious."

"I went to the hospital to see him last night, and I think he's in a coma." Alice gasped at Betty's words.

"Poor Mark! How's he taking it?"

"As strong as an oak tree! He's reacting the way he did the ten years he served our church. Strong in his faith and an encouragement to everybody around him. Even though he's worried sick about Eddie, he's being a tower of strength to everyone—even Dr. Zane, who's so concerned because he doesn't know what else to do."

"I'll leave as soon as I can dress. Thanks for coming to tell me, Betty."

"Do you want to go back with me? I don't like to have you driving alone."

"No, I'll be fine."

The hundred-mile drive usually passed quickly for Alice, but in her anxiety for Eddie, she thought the trip would never end. Adding to the mental strain was the certainty that Mark and his family faced a situation now that she couldn't fix. Had she been guilty of considering her money a panacea for everything? If she had, Alice knew now that all her money wasn't sufficient to save Eddie's life. If the best doctors in Richmond were stumped, there was nothing Alice Larkin could do. "When all else fails, pray." Was she the type of person who believed that? Did her security depend upon the fortune John had left her?

"God, forgive me," she muttered aloud. "I can't be Miss Fix-It anymore. I admit defeat— I can't make Eddie well, but You can. Please keep Mark from suffering the death of his son."

Admitting her own inadequacy and turning Eddie over to God calmed Alice's fears. She turned on the tape player and listened to the words of the Bible that she always played when she traveled alone. The narrator read from the book of Luke, and after listening for a half hour to the miraculous works of Jesus, she took particular note of the words, "But Jesus...healed the boy and gave him back to his father. And they were all amazed at the greatness of God."

Was this her assurance that Eddie would recover? Alice didn't know, but she had learned a needed lesson. Alice Larkin was a finite person who had little power to do anything; only God could be called great!

Alice had passed Richmond Children's Hospital several times during the months she lived in the city, but she hadn't been inside the building. The receptionist was helpful, and soon Alice stood before the closed door behind which she would find Eddie. Her hand trembled when she turned the doorknob and walked in without warning.

Eddie was lying, eyes closed, still as death, in the bed—his body small and frail under the thin sheet. Mark knelt by the bed, his head in his hands; Kristin and Gran sat nearby, their hands clasped.

When Alice saw how terrible Eddie looked, she started sobbing. Mark lifted his head, saw her grief, and rushed to her side.

"Oh, sweetheart, don't cry. He may get well—we can't tell yet," Mark said, and Alice sensed Mark's strength that Betty had mentioned. No faltering, no indecision anymore. Mark Tanner had recovered his faith in God and his purpose in life.

"I love him so much," Alice sobbed. "He can't die."

During most of their relationship, Alice had always been the one who'd comforted Mark, but Mark had become the protector now, and how good it was to lean on his strength!

Kristin tugged at Alice's hand. "Don't cry, Alice," but tears were pouring from her eyes, and Alice left Mark's embrace to kneel beside Kristin. She wiped Kristin's tears. "I'm sorry I was away when this happened."

"We've missed you so much—you always make things better."

"Mark," Gran called excitedly. "Eddie is moving."

"Maybe the sound of your voice brought him around," Mark said, as they all gathered around the bed. "Talk to him, Alice."

Alice perched on the bed, took Eddie's right hand,

careful not to dislodge any of the tubes connected to his little body. She caressed his face and brushed back the curls that had fallen over his forehead.

"Eddie," she whispered. "I've come to see you. Won't you wake up and talk to me?" She bent over and kissed him.

Mark's hand gripped Alice's shoulder. Slowly, Eddie licked his lips. His eyes fluttered a little, finally opened, and they brightened when he recognized her.

"Alice," he whispered, and the weakness in his voice distressed her. "I've missed you."

Alice heard a sob escape Mark's lips, and she lifted her fingers and covered his hand on her shoulder.

"I was only gone a few days."

"It seemed like a long time. I don't like to go home from school when you're not there. Aunt Margaret is fun, but I wanted you."

"You hurry and get well, and I'll be waiting when you get home from school."

"Alice, I've been asleep for a long time and I've been dreaming a lot. One time, I dreamed I was talking to Jesus, and he took me by the hand and told me He would show me my new mommy. And it was you, Alice—it was you! He wants you and Daddy to get married."

Overcome, Alice slumped on the bed beside him, and everyone cried except Eddie. Mark put his arm around Alice. "We won't wait any longer, Son. As soon as you're well enough to come to the wedding, I'll give you a new mama."

Eddie was released from the hospital a few days later, still weak, but definitely on the mend. Each night, Alice stayed at the hospital with the boy, so that Mark could continue his work, because his resignation would soon be effective, and he wanted to meet his obligations before then.

He was able to sit at the table and eat his meal the first night he came home. Alice watched him anxiously even though the doctors had assured her that he was out of danger. Mark went upstairs with Eddie and kept him company for an hour, but before he went to sleep, Eddie asked for Alice.

"Are you going to sit with me tonight?" he asked.

"I don't believe that's necessary. Your daddy will be right down the hall, and he'll be listening for you to call if you have trouble. Also, I'll leave my bedroom door open and you can ring your bell if you need me. I'll check on you again before I go to bed."

"What're you going to do until then? Why don't you stay with me?"

"Because I've been spending every night with you for over a week and I've had no time with Mark. Daddies need to know you love them, too."

"All right," Eddie said, "but you will come back before you go to bed?"

"You can count on it." Alice bent over and kissed his soft hair.

Mark waited at the bottom of the stairs. He put his arm around her, and they went into the family room and sat together on the couch.

"When can we get married?" Mark said.

"The sooner the better," Alice answered with a smile. "The doctor said that Eddie can go back to school in a week, so any time after that."

"Do you want a big wedding?"

Alice shook her head emphatically. "No. Let's go

to Tyler Memorial and have a short ceremony with only a few friends and relatives.''

Mark hesitated. ''Since I'm returning to the church as their pastor, I believe the members will be disappointed if they aren't invited to come. We could have the current pastor perform a simple ceremony, without fancy clothes or attendants, but invite anyone who wants to come.''

''You're right, of course—I hadn't thought of it that way. Will your parents come?''

''I'm sure they will, if my sister has time to look after the business.''

''My family will want to attend too, so we'll have several relatives.''

Mark stretched out his long legs and relaxed beside her.

''I've been so worried over the past few weeks that I wondered if I could ever be happy again. And now, you're here in my arms, and Eddie is upstairs asleep in his own bed.'' He drew her head down on his shoulder, and caressed her hair.

''Mark, I want to legally adopt Kristin and Eddie. I don't want to be a stepmother—I want to be their *mother*. Do you think they'll mind, or do you object?''

He laughed lowly. ''Why would I object? You're paying me a compliment to adopt my children so they will be 'ours.' That's wonderful, but what if we have a child? That would put Kristin and Eddie on the same legal basis as your child, and, considering your assets, that's a significant decision.''

''That's one of the reasons I want to adopt them.''

As soon as the wedding was over, Eddie started calling Alice, Mama, but the matter of how to address Alice seemed to be a major problem for Kristin. For several days, she didn't call her anything, but one evening when she was helping Alice prepare the evening meal, and they were alone in the kitchen, she said, "Why can't I call you 'Mother'?"

"I'd be happy to have you call me 'Mother.'"

"Mama sounds too babyish, and besides that's what I called my other mother." Alice was gratified that she didn't say "my *real* mother."

"I prefer to be called Mother, rather than Mom, so that sounds like a good choice."

Alice didn't report the conversation to Mark, but the first time he heard Kristin address her as "Mother," he lifted his eyebrows, and his dimple deepened. He was pleased.

When Alice awakened on the Sunday morning that Mark was to preach the first sermon of his renewed pastorate, her husband was seated in a chair near the window, a Bible in his hand. She sat up in bed, and he turned toward her. "I didn't mean to interrupt your meditations. Shall I go back to sleep?"

"No, come join me," Mark said, and he held out his arm to her. She slipped on a robe and went to sit on his knee.

"Nervous?" she asked.

"No. I've prepared my sermon well, and I've been praying just now for the Spirit's leadership when I face my congregation. It's strange that even though I was their pastor for years, it still seems like a beginning."

Alice caressed his face, feeling the roughness of his beard beneath the fair skin.

"I'm looking forward to hearing your sermon, and I know you'll do great. But we'd better get a move on if we want to get our whole family gussied up for the day. We don't want you to be ashamed of our appearance."

After a quick breakfast, while Mark helped the children to dress, Alice went across the hall to see if Gran needed any assistance.

The older woman was struggling to put on her stockings. "I'm getting slower all the time, Alice. I can't be ready in time."

"I'll help you. Mark is taking care of the kids." Alice knelt before her and pulled on the hose, then she lifted a dress over the older woman's head and secured the zipper.

"I wish I had a new dress, since this is such an important occasion, but I haven't bought anything for a long time."

"I'll take you shopping someday soon, so you can buy new clothing, and you might find some new items under the Christmas tree."

Gran patted Alice's hand. "You're good to me, Alice, as much as if I were your own grandmother, but I'm a burden to you. I think it would be better if I just go into a nursing home when you move."

Alice laid her arm around the angular, stooped shoulders.

"Gran, when I said 'I do' to Mark, I said 'I do' to his family. You're family, and unless you get completely disabled to the place that I can't take care of you, you're welcome to stay with us. So stop fretting about it. You're the nearest relative the children have, except their father, and it's important for them to have some ties to the past."

Alice had bought new clothes for Mark and the children in honor of this special occasion. Kristin wore a burnt-orange sweater with a brown skirt. Eddie had on a pair of blue trousers, a white shirt, and a light-blue silk tie. And Gran, in spite of her disability, presented a neat and gracious appearance in an aqua woolen dress. Before her stroke, she'd been above average in height, and Alice believed that in her youth, Gran had been a beauty.

Alice didn't have new clothes, but she dressed in the most expensive wool suit she'd ever owned. She'd bought it on sale a few months before she'd met Mark and his family. Mark whistled when Alice pirouetted in front of him for inspection. With the dark-brown suit, she wore a pink blouse that emphasized her pink-and-white complexion. She put on coral pendant earrings and fastened a matching brooch to her suit lapel.

Kristin and Eddie came running in the room and lined up beside Alice. "Do you think your family will do you credit today?" Alice asked. "We don't want you to be ashamed of us."

"I wouldn't be ashamed of you if you wore rags," he said. He knelt to hug Kristin and Eddie.

"Daddy, be careful—you'll muss my clothes," Kristin said as she backed away, but Eddie threw himself into his father's arms. When Mark stood, he took a long look at Alice, and hugged her so tightly that she squealed.

"Maybe I don't want to be mussed, either," she teased, but he only squeezed her harder. With his lips close to her ear, he whispered, "I don't deserve you. You're the best thing that's ever happened to me."

Alice and her family were ushered to a front seat in the crowded sanctuary. When Mark entered and took his seat on the platform, his eyes searched the congregation until he found them. He smiled broadly and surveyed the other worshipers with a sweeping glance. There were no empty seats, and the ushers were scurrying around trying to seat latecomers in the balcony.

"I want to thank you for calling me as your pastor, giving me a second chance to take up the cross I'd laid down," Mark said in his opening remarks. He read the text for the sermon.

"'But one thing I do: Forgetting what is behind and straining toward what is ahead, I press on toward the goal to win the prize for which God has called me heavenward in Christ Jesus.'" When she heard the text, Alice surmised that his sermon would be a personal testimony.

Since this was the first time Alice had heard Mark preach, she tried to be objective in her appraisal, and that was difficult to achieve when her heart was stirred at his physical appearance. He was more robust now than he'd been when she'd first met him, his color was better, and his erect stature hinted of strength and confidence. His voice was deep and compassionate, and he spoke with an authority and firmness that kept the audience's attention.

"Oh, God," Alice prayed inwardly, "thank You for Your perseverance in bringing Him back to You and Your service."

In a trembling voice, he told of the trying days during the illness of his son and wife. "I let my troubles overwhelm me, and for months I neglected the ministry I'd been called to. I was in the depth of despair when I cried to God, like David of old, asking Him to 'bring me out of the slimy pit, out of the mud and mire, and set my feet on a rock and give me a firm place to stand.' That's when He sent Alice to our home as a nanny for the children. She encouraged all of us to a higher plane of living, and the fact that I'm back in the place God wants me to be is due primarily to Alice, whom I married a month ago.''

A hush settled over the sanctuary—he held everyone's attention.

''This time last year, I'd never heard of Alice. Some of you know what our situation was like when she came to us in May, and if you compare it to our home life today, you'd understand why I'm so grateful to Alice and why I love her so much. She's been God's instrument to work a miracle in our lives.''

Mark discussed his personal goals, his aspirations for the church, and how he had submitted his life totally to the will of God.

After he completed his sermon and had the closing song, Mark paused significantly. ''I feel that it's necessary for me to once again refer to a personal matter, which I will never mention before this congregation again. It's no secret that there has been some question about my morality in the past few months, and I'm happy that all of those matters have been cleared up, and any ill will between me and others has been completely resolved. I can't have scandal soiling my life if I'm to serve God the way I intend to.''

Alice couldn't help wonder if it was wise for Mark to broach this subject, and it embarrassed her, but on the other hand, this public announcement of his feelings toward her might set to rest, once and for all, any question about their past relationship.

"Until I met Alice, I didn't suppose that there was any woman who could epitomize the wife cited in the last chapter of Proverbs, but I believe that Alice does. I want to read a few select verses from that portion of Scripture, and if you other men feel about your wives as I do about mine, reach out and take their hands as I read.

"A wife of noble character who can find? She is worth far more than rubies. Her husband has full confidence in her and lacks nothing of value. She brings him good and not harm, all the days of her life…. She opens her arms to the poor and extends her hands to the needy…. She is clothed in strength and dignity; she can laugh at the days to come…. She watches over the affairs of her household and does not eat the bread of idleness. Her children arise and call her blessed."

Two little hands reached for hers, and Alice thanked God for her family, as Mark continued to read.

"Her husband also, and he praises her: Many women do noble things, but you surpass them all. Charm is deceptive, and beauty is fleeting; but a woman who fears the Lord is to be praised."

When he finished reading, Mark held out a beckoning hand to Alice, and she joined him in front of the congregation. Mark hugged her tightly with one arm, the huge audience rose to its feet, and applause resounded throughout the room.

Mark and Alice had been accepted, and they publicly committed themselves to a life of service.

Epilogue

Alice stood in the large hallway and watched as Kristin came down the stairway, wearing Clarice's wedding gown, which Alice has preserved carefully for this day. She kissed her daughter when she reached the bottom of the stairs.

"Thanks, Mother, for giving me this beautiful wedding. You've been so good to all of us, and I hope I can be as good a wife and mother as you've been."

Alice's throat was too tight for words, but she went with Kristin to the rear door where Mark waited for her. In his black tuxedo, he was more handsome than ever. In ten years, most of his hair had turned a beautiful gray, with only a few dark streaks to remind her how he'd looked when she first entered his Richmond home.

Mark wanted the privilege of escorting his firstborn to the improvised altar they'd arranged in the white gazebo of their elegant flower garden. His associate minister would conduct the first part of the ceremony, but Mark would take the vows of Kristin and the young man she'd chosen.

As she watched them, Alice was suddenly swept off her feet.

"Stop it, Eddie," she cried, as he swung her high and planted a big kiss on the back of her neck, a habit he'd started when he became as tall as she was. When he released her, he grinned, his blue eyes sparkling. "I thought it was customary to kiss the mother of the bride."

Alice kissed his cheek, her heart overflowing with love for this boy who'd been such an important part of her life.

Eddie offered his arm and escorted Alice to her seat and joined the minister and groom to wait for the bride. Looking at Eddie's broad shoulders, she could hardly envision him as the sickly, scrawny kid he used to be. Although only a high school junior, he was already under consideration for scholarships by many colleges due to his track record.

Some melancholy mingled with her happiness as Alice watched her family gather. The ten years had not all been easy—Mark had undergone many crises in his ministry; during his childhood, Eddie had several physical relapses; and Kristin had often been rebellious. But time had a way of healing the hurts and problems, and during it all, the love she and Mark shared had never wavered.

Alice noticed Grover Tatum and his family in the group of assembled guests, many standing on the outside of the picket fence when the seats were filled. After Alice had saved his son, Tatum and his family had returned to the church's fellowship, and he'd become one of Mark's most vocal supporters.

The organist started the processional and Alice turned slightly to watch the wedding party. Susie, Kristin's longtime friend from Richmond, was the maid of honor, followed by seven-year-old Melissa, who took seriously her role as flower girl. Dressed in a pale-pink dainty dress that set off her blond features, she was almost an exact image of what Alice had been at that age. As Melissa took her place before the altar, Mark and Alice exchanged glances, and he smiled.

Alice knew that he, too, had remembered the day she'd bolted into his church office, although she never bothered him when he was on duty there. When she saw Mark, she'd burst into tears, and he'd rounded the desk immediately to take her in his arms.

"Why, sweetheart, what's the matter?"

Swallowing a sob, she said, "I'm pregnant. We're going to have a baby."

Mark was silent for a few moments. "And that makes you unhappy?"

She shook her head back and forth on his shoulder. "No. No. I'm happy. I've wanted to have your baby, but I'd given up—I decided I couldn't have children."

Mark drew her even closer in his arms and laughed in his low, chuckling way.

"I couldn't be happier. I want a daughter just like you." And he'd gotten what he wanted.

A trumpet blast rolled from the organ, and Alice turned her attention from Melissa. This was Kristin's day, and she was sorry that Clarice wasn't here to see the child she'd borne, and that Gran, who'd died, peaceful and happy in their home three years ago, couldn't have lived to see this day. Except for Mark,

Melissa and Eddie, Kristin had no blood relatives with her today, but strangely, it didn't seem to matter to the girl. Not only had Alice adopted Mark's children; they had adopted her and her relatives as well, and all of Alice's family had come today, as well as Ethel Pennington, now happily married, who'd remained like an aunt to Eddie and Kristin.

While the wedding guests enjoyed a full meal at the long tables set up by the caterers on the front lawn, Alice posed for pictures with her family. She surveyed the magnificent antebellum home she'd provided for them. They'd been happy here, and she prayed that they might have many more years to enjoy it.

Although all eyes were on Kristin, Mark put his arm around Alice. "She's a beautiful bride," he whispered, "but not the most beautiful woman here today. You know who that is."

"You've always been a bit prejudiced, but I like it that way."

"I wonder what the future holds for us?" Mark said speculatively.

"It doesn't matter as long as we're together, does it?"

Mark answered with a soft kiss on her lips.

* * * * *

Dear Reader,

Although my characters are often affluent, I don't want to come across as a person who believes that riches ultimately bring happiness, for in many cases, wealth can have a detrimental effect on a relationship. While I try to create characters who overcome their conflicts by means of personal attributes and spiritual beliefs, I also like to portray rich people who are good stewards of their money, using it to improve the lives of others.

I believe the Bible teaches that Christians are expected to share their money with those less fortunate than themselves. I've been a tither since I had my first job when I was fifteen, and it's always a pleasure for my husband and me to contribute at least ten percent of our income to spread the Gospel. We've been blessed financially and spiritually because we keep the Lord's command: "Bring the whole tithe into the storehouse, that there may be food in my house. Test me in this, says the Lord Almighty, and see if I will not throw open the floodgates of heaven and pour out so much blessing that you will not have room enough for it." (*Malachi* 3:10)

Wealth can be a blessing or a curse, but my characters have made riches a blessing because they portray the Scriptural words, "It is more blessed to give than to receive." (*Acts* 20:35)

I will be happy to hear from my readers at the following address: P.O. Box 2770, Southside, WV 25187.

Irene B. Brand

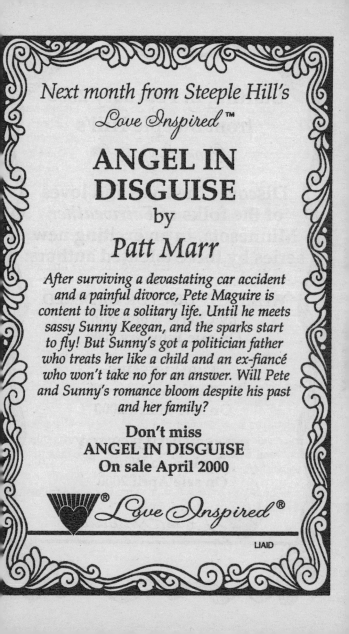